THE
NEW
WORLD

THE NEW WORLD

CHRIS ADRIAN *and* ELI HOROWITZ

GRANTA

Granta Publications, 12 Addison Avenue, London W11 4QR

First published in Great Britain by Granta Books, 2015
First published in the United States by Farrar, Straus and Giroux,
New York, 2015

A CIP catalogue record for this book is available from the British
Library.

1 3 5 7 9 10 8 6 4 2

ISBN 978 1 78378 210 9 (hardback)
ISBN 978 1 78378 212 3 (ebook)

Offset by Avon DataSet Ltd, Bidford-on-Avon, Warwickshire

Printed and bound by CPI Group (UK) Ltd, Croydon, CR0 4YY

For Rachel and Jason and Shirley and Larry

CYCLE ONE

CYCLE ONE

1

Jim collapsed and died at the hospital where he and Jane both worked, she as a pediatric surgeon and he as a chaplain—a humanist chaplain, as he liked to remind everyone. Jane was on a flight home from a conference in Paris, fast asleep in transatlantic tranquillity. After the plane landed, her phone stumbled over itself, the notifying chimes and vibrations interrupting each other as soon as she turned it on. There was a message from Jim, sent hours ago. So she was tricked, for half a second, into thinking he was fine. Then she saw all the other texts, and all the voice mails. Jane's seatmate, a hair-helmeted blond lady, laid a hand on Jane's arm and said, "Oh, something terrible has happened, hasn't it?"

"My husband is sick," Jane said, though she already believed, from the volume and tone of the messages, that he must be dead. While Jane tried to return every call, her seatmate pushed with her through the cab line at JFK, yelling, "Out of the way! Can't you people see this is an *emergency*?"

No one picked up, not even Jane's mother. "Why isn't anyone answering?" she asked her seatmate calmly as they came to the head of the line. This was Jane's version of hysteria. Another person might already be weeping and shouting or rolling in silent anguish on the sidewalk, knowing what Jane knew, but she only mumbled at a stranger and kept walking forward.

"I just don't know, honey," the lady said, and then she was opening the cab door and gently pushing Jane in. The lady gave the driver stern instructions, then came back to press her palm earnestly against the window. Jane pressed her hand to the glass as well. *She, too, must have a dead husband,* Jane said to herself, because it seemed so much like a gesture of solidarity.

"Can't you go any faster?" Jane asked, once the cab was on the highway. "It's an emergency. My husband is very ill."

"I am so sorry," the driver said, shrugging and indicating the traffic with his hands.

"I'm sorry, too," Jane said, and stared at her phone for a few more minutes before she asked, "Don't you have a light or a siren?" It made such sense to her in that moment—people had emergencies in taxis all the time. Babies were born in taxis. One had been born somewhere on the BQE just the other week. "For emergencies?"

"No," the driver said gently. "We are not allowed."

"That's too bad," she said, leaning her head against the window. She imagined rolling it down and making a wailing siren of her mouth and her head, and she could see the cartoon image very clearly—her neck stretched impossibly long and her eyes flashing and spinning, one red and one blue, her lips oversize and overdefined, wrapping sensuously around every howling O up the Grand Central Parkway and clearing a path. "Now we are making better time," the driver said, and "Now we are making *good* time," and "Now we are almost there!" even when they weren't. Jane didn't say anything else. When they finally did arrive, she pushed some money at him without counting it and went inside. Striding carefully toward one of the resuscitation bays, she tried to keep her face solemn and still, though it felt like something—phantom fingers or two blunt fists—was pushing at her lips and cheeks to force them into a terrified, snarling smile.

For a moment she thought Jim must still be alive, because she recognized a vigorous code when she saw one. She even detected a note of hopefulness in all the bustle, before she saw the wife in the corner of the room, before she saw the patient's single square toe visible through the surrounding bodies, and before she understood that she had just presented herself as the star of somebody else's emergency. The toe was dark brown. The widow-in-waiting, getting harassed or comforted by the chaplain, was a tall Asian lady with sunglasses pushed back on her head. "Jane!" said the chaplain, a colleague of her husband's named Dick. The ER attending at the head of the bed called out her name as well. Jane backed out of the room waving her hands in some gesture she had never made before, meant to represent an apology particular to the horror and farce of the situation. She collided with

Maureen, her surgical colleague and friend, who turned her around and embraced her.

"Holy shit, Jane," she said, but gently. "Holy *shit*!"

"What happened?" Jane asked, pulling away. "Where is he?" Dick was fluttering behind her, but she wasn't listening to whatever he was saying.

"It was a saddle embolism," Maureen said. "He's upstairs. They closed off part of recovery for you."

"Recovery? He was in surgery? Someone took it out? Who did it? Who tried?"

"Not that. It was too late for that." Maureen led her away down the hall to stand in the charting area, where everyone within distance of ordinary hearing quietly got up and walked away. Dick was still aflutter, repeatedly touching his lips and his heart, and now Jane could hear him saying her name and Jim's over and over. She put a hand on him to make him still and another on Maureen, clutching hard at her biceps. "It was the Polaris people," Maureen said. "They were already here for someone else, so they took him while he was still on bypass."

"The who people? Took him where? To surgery?"

"Polaris. The *cryo* people. Holy shit, Jane. I *assisted*. I feel like I should apologize, but I figured you would want someone to make sure they didn't fuck it up."

"Fuck what up? *What are you talking about?*"

"Oh, Jesus," Maureen said, trying to back away, but Jane wouldn't let her go. "You don't know?"

"It's what I've been *saying* about the *surprise*," Dick murmured, stroking Jane's hand. "He didn't tell me, either. But in a way, in a really particular way, something *wonderful* has happened."

"What?" Jane said, and then she was shouting again, and she could not understand what they were saying to her, no matter how plainly they told it, until they led her to Jim's body (and it was definitely his body, for she uncovered it and immediately recognized his fat pink nipples, his round belly, and his short legs and stubby, hairy toes) and showed her how the Polaris people, whoever they were, had taken away his head.

2

In darkness, he understood these words: *Greetings and salutations!* Except the words were not exactly spoken, and Jim did not exactly hear them. Once upon a time he had wondered aggressively what it would be like to hear voices, and tried to imagine his way into the head of the psychiatry patients who always insisted that the boxes of tissues or the window blinds were piteously weeping and who asked, when he tried to pray with them, why no one ever wanted to minister to the inanimate, who needed and wanted it more than most of the living could ever know or understand. *Is this what that's like?* he asked himself now, realizing, as he asked this one, that there were other, more pressing questions. So, in the absence of a mouth and a tongue, in the absence of air, he asked, *Am I alive?*

You have always been alive, he was told. *But now you are awake.*

He remembered, in a very remote and stale way, a

great panic at dying, and asking someone—not God, of course—for just a few more minutes, and he remembered how he had understood in his body that he wasn't going to get them. Much fresher than the memory of dying was a memory of terrible, terrible pain, and he tried to decide whether he had simply been dreaming of pain, or if it was agony to come back to life, or if the pain of dying could not abate if you never actually died, or if he had simply been in some kind of Hell. He supposed it didn't matter, so he decided not to ask.

Who are you? Jim asked. *Where am I? Why can't I see you?*

There are short answers and long answers to all those questions. Which would you prefer to hear? There is time for either or both.

Let's start with the short ones.

I am your (social worker). You are at (Polaris). And you are not trying hard enough to see me.

(Social worker)? Jim asked.

Yes. It is a word you know, but it does not entirely suit the present context. Hence (social worker).

(Polaris)? You mean, it worked?

Of course.

It really worked? I'm really alive?

You have always been alive.

He thought to himself, *I am alive!*, very subtly aware, in this new state of being, how thinking to himself was different from (speaking). Alive in the future! How about that? He waited some period of time—it was hard to tell if it was a minute or a month—to feel excited or exultant, but the notion of life remained only supremely *interesting.*

But am I all here? I don't feel entirely like myself. Or am I on some kind of drug, maybe a tranquilizer? Because I'm in the hospital?

You are not on drugs. Neither are you in a hospital. But you are here and not here. Right now, you are only the leaven of your connectome.

My what?

Your connectome. The totality of your neurological connections. Your quantum self.

I don't think I understand.

Of course you don't. We are getting ahead of ourselves.

I see. He paused another (moment). *And why can't I see anything? Did you tell me that I'm not trying hard enough to see you?*

I did tell you that. But I should have said not trying at all. There is a short and a long solution to that problem. Would you like the short solution first?

Yes, please.

The short solution is try harder.

Try harder? Like to wake up?

You were never asleep. You won't fully understand until you make your (Debut).

My (Debut)? Like cotillion? Or like on Broadway?

It is the culmination of the third and final cycle by which the leaven of your connectome expands to inhabit every space of your personality within a new body, learns and forgets what it must know and cannot know to live in the future, and joins with us in fellowship. The sequence is thus: (Incarnation); (Examination); (Debut).

I don't understand!

Yes. There you go again.

Getting ahead of ourselves?

Indeed. You should ignore everything but the one thing. Do you remember what that one thing is?

Trying harder? To see you?

Yes, exactly.

Jim noted the absence of eyelids to shut tight, or hands to squeeze into fists, or buttocks and a jaw to clench—everything he was accustomed to doing when he was really trying at something. Instead, he tried to muster their interior equivalents, opening a door in his mind onto scenes of struggle: squats and jerks and lifting a corner of the refrigerator, and arguments with the head of the hospital about funding for the Clinical Pastoral Education program, all times when he was full to bursting with what he wanted. And yet all of these interior equivalents felt, as he deployed them, like they were not enough. He tried another sort of effort—it felt like what he did when he was praying as hard as he could, which he had once described to a nonhumanist chaplain who had expressed doubt that somebody who didn't believe in God could pray, as an effort like *internal pooping.* That was better, divorced, as it was, from physical effort, which was clearly the wrong thing to bring to bear on this situation. But now, instead of having a general sense of being suspended in darkness that was neither warm nor cold but without any temperature at all, Jim was falling.

Falling became an occasion for panic, but it also offered him a first lesson in how he must proceed. He wished he had taken a little more time just to chat with his (social worker), since it was clear to him that he was failing now *because* he was trying, falling only because he had conceived of the space through which he could fall. He thought of a rope, and there it was, at once an idea and a mental object. The rope wasn't enough to stop him falling—he slipped from knot to knot to knot. But now he had shown himself the distance between try and do, and offered himself a solution: if he wanted to *see* her, he must *conceive* of her. Except what he really meant was (conceive), since what seemed called for was a different kind of thinking and conceiving, a different kind of mental effort, than he was used to, some kind never needed before by anybody and so at the very least unused throughout the history of man, if not actually uncreated. And if this was the short solution to his problem, Jim was suddenly afraid of finding out what the long one might be.

But then, as he was (grasping) the last knot on his rope, there came a flash of light. It was exactly the sort of light that explodes in your interior perception when you stand up into an open cabinet and smack your head, or someone punches you in the eyeball. He pulled himself up, quickly exhausting not just the rope but the very idea of pulling. He (moved) into notions of pushing and twisting and thrusting, and from there to notion-motions for which he had no name except (dance): tense, generative gestures that seemed to create not just the space but the sheltering dimensions through which he traveled.

And each gesture was part of a loud, conscious fuss over enormous concepts: *NO, I don't want to die* and *YES, let me see your face, let me see your body and my body* and *LET ME SEE THIS NEW WORLD!* There was color in the light, and then the light and color bled profusely, establishing and populating Jim's whole field of vision.

He was outside, on a farm. There was the house, and the barn, and the silo, and the big blue bowl of sky with clouds in the shape of elephants and castles and whales. What a beautiful world! And there was his new friend— he thought she looked beautiful before he thought she looked strange—sitting patiently above him at the center of a silvery web, waving four arms and blinking at him with very tiny but truly luminous blue eyes.

Greetings and salutations! she said.

3

Jane's reverend mother presided over Jim's funeral, which was not at all the service he had asked for. Jane barely had attention for any of the details, but she was peripherally aware of her mother shouting at Jim's friends when they called to complain. Jim had wanted a pagan Viking service, complete with basso chanting and a flammable boat set alight with a fire arrow as it drifted away from the mourners. Instead of that, her mother had arranged a Unitarian Universalist service heavily inflected with her native Congregational elements, though Jane's mother said over and over to Jim's friends that she would keep mention of Jesus to a minimum. Once Jane talked briefly with Dick—he called just as she picked up the phone to continue her assault on Polaris Cryonics Incorporated. "We all *promised* him," Dick had said. "You promised him it would be a certain way, and now you are breaking your promise."

"Well," Jane had replied, "he broke a promise, too, didn't he?" She meant his marriage vows, one of which had been, at Jim's own insistence, that the two of them would remain together *beyond death*. At first that just meant they would be eternity to each other. Then, later, Jane understood it to mean they would cleave to each other beyond the efforts of their individual griefs (past, present, and future) to drive them apart. Which their griefs did try to do, over and over, and yet the two of them always managed (sometimes triumphantly, she would like to say) to muddle through. *Always together, never apart* was what they had promised, even if they never quite permanently vanquished their respective intimacy issues. But now Jane was quite sure that remaining together *beyond death* meant nothing at all if it didn't mean that neither of them would sign up alone for an afterlife—and never mind that it was as fake and stupid as any scheme of ordinary religion. The whole terrible surprise of this Polaris Incident, as her mother liked to call it, felt somehow like Jim had left her for somebody else, like infidelity added to death. If she thought for a minute that he would understand, Jane might have tried to tell these things to Dick, before her mother took the phone away from her and hung up on him.

Jane stood for the hymns during the service but did not sing. Her aunt Millicent, who had arrived, as always, in tow with her mother, warbled prettily beside her, her voice very much like her sister's, but without the confidence, strength, or control. Millicent had been out of her mind with dementia for almost five years. "As the deer panteth for the water," she sang, smiling, "so my soul longeth after thee!" When she saw Jane looking at her, she winked, and Jane thought, *Exactly—this whole thing is a practical joke.* She knew already from her work—because her young patients sometimes died—how the world could seem unreal to the bereaved. That was something Jim used to talk about all the time, how he had spent the afternoon on the moons of Jupiter or in darkest Narnia, when he meant he had been professionally immersed in somebody else's grief. It was all supposed to seem unreal or impossible, but it wasn't supposed to be ridiculous.

"Do you mean to tell me," Jane had asked Brian, the Polaris customer service representative, "that you think what you did was legal?"

"Of course, Dr. Cotton." He had a quality to his voice that she would describe to her mother as *furry*, meaning that when she tried to picture what he looked like she could only visualize a teddy bear, its face stuck in a stupid sympathetic half-smile. "Can you imagine that we would offer our service if it wasn't?"

"Oh, I'm sure it's legal in *Florida*," she said. "But that doesn't mean it's right. That doesn't mean I won't have the health department come confiscate every last drop of liquid nitrogen in your filthy buckets."

"We call them dewars. And, Dr. Cotton, I just want to tell you that everything you're feeling is perfectly normal."

"Normal?" she said, and then she shouted, "I don't think you people are allowed to use that word!"

At the funeral, they sang "Abide with Me" and "When We Were Living" and listened to a succession of eulogies. Jane's mother had sat up all night writing a sermon on the death of Abigail Adams, in which she expounded upon the gifts of time and silence, but it was Dick and his friends, who sat in a block and wore Viking helmets, who gave most of the speeches, telling stories—each one felt more endless than the last—about Jim at work and at play.

Jane tried not to listen to any of the eulogies, because it felt like all the speakers were conspiring to make her break down. Now she appreciated how fire arrows and a hurly match and Renaissance fair turkey legs and even the burning boat and burning body would be easier to deal with than this train of perfectly sincere people who wielded their affectionate memories of Jim like heavy cudgels, all aimed directly at her face. And how many times could somebody hit you in the face before you started to cry?

Millicent was lifting her dress by slow inches and looking slyly around the crowded church. She rarely disrobed completely, but she liked to flash her panties. Jane gently smoothed the dress down over Millicent's lap, then pulled her aunt's head to her shoulder. Dick had ascended the pulpit to imagine out loud the wonders of the future into which Jim would wake. He told them all not to be sad, because Jim wasn't *really* dead: when you thought about it, he had just undertaken a truly remarkable *journey*. Dick confessed he'd been just as astonished as anyone that Jim had arranged to take this particular journey, but wasn't that exactly the gift he had left them all, the very good news that every one of them could follow their dear friend into the future and *be with him forever?* He said more, but Jane plugged her ears and leaned forward, trying to look funeral-casual, as if she were overwhelmed with sadness rather than anger and disgust. She did not stand up and shout, *That's not how it was supposed to be!* She and Jim were going to be together forever in oblivion, and now this fool was inviting the whole church to an imaginary afterlife that Jane wouldn't have any part in.

"It's a mistake," she had told Brian. "You have to understand. He wouldn't have believed in what you do. I know he wouldn't. He didn't believe in anything but *right now.*"

"I know it must be a shock," Brian said. "And I'm very sorry. It's a very common reaction. I can tell you you're not the first spouse that's been surprised like this."

"It's not what he *believed*," Jane said, as if Brian simply hadn't heard her. "And what you're talking about isn't even possible. So, please, just tell me what I have to do to get his head back from you."

"I'm sorry, Dr. Cotton," he'd said. "What you're asking for—*that's* not possible. The way we understand the situation, that would be like killing him. Do you see what I mean?"

She did not see. Or rather, all she could see when she tried was Jim's head frozen in a block of water, an enormous novelty ice cube. Or she saw his head being lowered by the hair into a bubbling and spitting pool of liquid nitrogen, then accidentally dropped on a marble floor, his features scattering every which way in shards. Or she saw his pale bloodless face suspended in a tall jar of blue barbershop disinfectant, eyes lifeless but not blank, still full of horror at how he had fallen for a bait and switch. She demanded proof that they had actually done what they had been contracted to do, that they hadn't just wrapped his head in toilet paper and tossed it out in the hospital trash.

"Of course," Brian said. "We maintain full video documentation of the vitrification process." And while Polaris wasn't required by any law to show that to her, they certainly would, if she wanted them to. Did she want them to?

He waited very patiently while she failed to answer, not hanging up or even asking if she was still there. And when her silence transitioned to quiet sobs, he waited even a little longer before he said, "I really am sorry, Dr. Cotton. I'm so sorry for your perceived loss."

4

She wasn't really a spider. Jim had not actually become a pig. They weren't really on a farm. It was a sort of staging area. A virtual (anteroom), as the spider revealed to him, shaped by the deeply embedded influences of his native culture and the inclinations of his recovering imagination. The client always started someplace comfortable and familiar.

Started? he asked. He was fancy-stepping in a circle in his pen.

Yes. She was busily weaving letters in her web. *It is the nature of one (antechamber) to give way to another as your (Incarnation) proceeds, as though through rooms, until you exit into the (real) world and go on to conduct your (Examination) and make your (Debut). Sometimes there are many rooms, sometimes there are just a few.* Jim pondered this while she finished her message: DELICIOUS PIG.

I don't think that's what it's supposed to say.

The spider shrugged her tiny gray shoulders.

Why (real), he asked, *and not just* real?

Now she frowned. *As before, there is a distance between what I understand by that word and what you understand by it.*

I'm not even sure what I understand.

It's not predominantly a matter of understanding. Would you like to move on to the next (anteroom)?

Oh, yes. Definitely. I don't want to spend the future as a pig.

Then take us there.

How do I do that? he asked. *Let's start with the short answer.*

You have already done it once.

But I'm not even sure of what I did, exactly. He paused, waiting for her to help him out somehow. *What did it look like to you?* he asked.

Well, she said, *it appeared to be a deployment of the right kind of curiosity and imagination. A forceful but effortless kind, if you know what I mean.*

I don't! he said, and then added, *Not (curiosity)? Not (imagination)?*

By these words, I mean what you mean and I understand what you understand. And she had woven a new message without him noticing: YOU CAN DO IT.

He set his adorable hooves firmly in the dirt, lowered his snout, and squinted.

Should I close my eyes?

I don't know.

He didn't ask for any more advice. Instead, he asked himself if he should try to make those two words—*curiosity* and *imagination*—into one word and *speak* them, or combine the ideas behind the words into a new word and *(speak)* that, or just strain wordlessly against the earth and the sky, demanding that this creation doff its mask and show him *what was really there*. He tried the last of these, straining and groaning, but nothing happened.

Try again.

Jim composed himself, pressing forward to shove his head between the boards of his stall. *Show me!* he demanded, and considered, quite vigorously, how almost all of what he knew about himself right now was his commitment to being alive in the real world of the future, and how desperately interested he was in this new world; his curiosity had the force of love or despair. A seed of feeling shuddered in him. He had a quick, unsettling thought of a woman, pale, dark-haired, and small, and put the memory aside, a distraction from the immediate, elusive challenge, but the accompanying spasm of energy powered him forward. In one hand he held his devotion to the future, and his curiosity about it in the other, and then it seemed to him that he needed a third hand, to hold the third thing, which was his desire to live. Then he remembered he had hoofs, not hands, and then he understood that he didn't really have hoofs—he was holding these ideas with some grasping device of his undying and omnipotent mind.

By a process that was physical and mental at the same time, he threw these three things at the substance of the world of the farm. *(Aha)!* he shouted, and suddenly the whole world seemed as fragile as it had been beautiful, everything, from the grass to the leaves to the clouds, as lustrous and vulnerable as richly colored glass. When it all broke apart, Jim seized the pieces and remade them. It was not effortless. Why had the spider said it would be effortless? It was exhausting.

Is this it? Jim asked. He was lying in a bed fit precisely for Louis XVI, with heavy white sheets pulled up to his chin. He held up his hands, spotted and wrinkled, in front of his face. *Is this the real world?* he asked.

No. Now she was human, dressed in a Pan Am flight suit and space turban. *But it is much closer.*

At least I'm not a pig, he said.

You are not a pig. She was holding a tray of food, liquid dinner boxes labeled with pictures of carrots and peas and pork. *Are you hungry?*

What's your name? he asked.

Alice is my name, she said.

Alice, he said hesitantly. *Do I know you?*

You knew part of me, once.

I did?

Yes. I conducted all Polaris phase two interviews beginning in January 2007.

Jim gasped. *I remember you—you're a robot!*

Not anymore, she said. *Are you hungry?*

Alice, Jim said, holding up his hands again. *What year is it?*

It is too early for me to answer that question for you.

But why?

That question also cannot be answered at the moment.

Jim sighed and put his face in his hands. *Well, what time is it, then? Can you tell what time it is?*

It is time for you to continue the work of (Incarnation), she said, carefully setting the tray down at her feet. Then she stepped closer to the bed, leaned over, and kissed him.

At first, Jim kept all his further questions to himself, and tried very hard just to concentrate. That wasn't easy at all, and later it felt like a significant accomplishment that he hadn't blurted out any of his initial thoughts—*Is it all right that I am having sex with my (social worker)? Do you have condoms in the future? Are we making love so you can conceive the body that I must inhabit here in the now?*—or that he hadn't made any of his anxieties visible and palpable. He worried that Alice would turn back into a spider and he would find himself suddenly forcing his tongue into her disgusting mouthparts, or that she would become a pig, or a piece of soft fruit, or an oven or a teakettle. He remembered, as he struggled, that he had had this problem before.

But though he was sure he kept his imagination quite still, everything changed. His body got younger by the minute—the spots disappeared from his hands and his droopy piebald scrotum became hairy and hale. His chest rose up higher toward his chin and his bottom tightened and strengthened with every thrust. Alice did not age either forward or backward, but her face, every time he lifted his head to look at her, was different under the pristine white turban, and then the turban was gone. She was bald, and then she had luxurious soft blond hair, then Nefertiti's Afro. She was white and black, yellow and green, purple and blue, and often alien though only ever in a sexy original-series *Star Trek* way; she was never anything but a female, and even though she sometimes had scalloped ridges on her forehead, or extra eyes or vaginas, or gently stinging tentacles in among her pubic hair, she tended, more and more as Jim edged close to orgasm, toward a very ordinary type of human woman, with black wavy hair and brown eyes, a big nose and a small, gentle mouth. Jim knew that he knew this face, though he was trying not to recognize it in exactly the way he was trying not to come.

The room kept changing as well. The bed was a bed, but then it was a boat, and then an altar, and then a casket lined with puffy satin before it was a bed again. The walls of the room were shining white, and then for a while they might be some new color, unknown to him, but always complementary to Alice's skin, before they became transparent or just disappeared—Jim was looking at them and then he was looking *through* them. But he paid closest attention to the action, at what his hands were doing and what his cock was doing—especially that. Sometimes he would slow down just to watch, and somebody would say, "Always together, never apart. Look at my face."

Did you say something? Jim asked.

I did not speak, Alice replied. In this moment, her nose was a beak but her mouth was a plump orange flower. He was aware that fantastic vistas of space lay now beyond the transparent or nonexistent walls, the moons of Jupiter and the rings of Saturn, starfields as thick as snowfields, patches of deep darkness subtly colored with blue energy.

Over the headboard he could see new stars and planets winking into existence at the crest of a propagating wave of creation, and it took only a few thrusts of his pelvis to understand what was driving that wave. This was merely the confirmation of something he'd always suspected or maybe even seen before in some masturbating flight of his imagination, tiny couples fucking at the heart of a clockwork to drive its gears, or arranged in pairs of four, six, or eight to make the cars go, or pushing the flowers from out of their fuses.

I am fucking the world into existence! he cried.

Not exactly true, Alice said, though not in a way that at all embarrassed him or dulled his ardor. *And not exactly false, either. But now is not the time to be explaining minor distinctions.*

(Fuck)! Jim cried, and certainly it felt like a generative word. It felt like he was using it correctly for the first time, like saying *Jesus!* when you saw Him in a piece of blackened toast, or *Oh, my God!* when a bush in your backyard happened spontaneously to burst into flame.

(Fuck)! he shouted again, and though he knew the future must be a perfect and perfectly happy place, he could not help but bring a little anguish into the world he was making. He said to himself, *Don't ruin this nice world by being anxious about absolutely nothing.* But then he heard the echo of another voice saying again, "Look at my face," and he understood the anguish was merely the herald of that ordinary face. Anguish drove his hips harder, and he was trying to make those ordinary features disappear, or trying to summon them permanently, or trying to push through the last soft black wall that kept his act of creation from propagating indefinitely, or

he was just trying to come, and that last eternal bit of effort reminded him, as always, of how the space between two people was almost unbridgeable, since sometimes— maybe even the best times—you had to work so impossibly hard to close it.

He came, as he expected, with a big bang, and finally that ordinary face opened its gentle mouth to give a cry that seemed almost all grief, and surely the reason Jim was crying out "Jane! Jane! Jane!" in sadness was because he was dying again (though in reverse, which was not at all the same thing as being born) and someone must sing him back into the world with laments.

But when Alice spoke at last it was in tones of quiet joy. "Congratulations," she said, a few moments or a million years later. "And welcome to the real world. Open your eyes now, and see it."

5

Two days after Jim's funeral, the mailman delivered a large triangular envelope to their house in Brooklyn. Jane studied the unopened envelope, which bore a Florida postmark and the Polaris logo at its peak, imagining it would contain a grotesque sympathy card, signed by everyone in the grotesque company and probably illustrated with some grotesque cartoon character—a penguin or a polar bear or an Eskimo or, most likely, a severed frozen Eskimo head that said, in a frosty word balloon, IN ESKIMO WE HAVE 1,000 WORDS FOR SNOW BUT ONLY ONE WORD FOR **THE FUTURE** or THERE WAS ONLY ONE PAIR OF FOOTPRINTS IN THE SNOW BECAUSE **THE FUTURE** WAS CARRYING ME THE WHOLE TIME or **THE FUTURE** IS SO SORRY FOR YOUR **PERCEIVED** LOSS.

But instead there was just a DVD in a blank sleeve, labeled on its face: *D.O.V.—Polaris Member 10.77.89.1.* The DVD was clipped to a glossy blue brochure, along with a note on a piece of Brian's stationery (his official title was Senior Vice President for Family Relations). *I wanted you to have a little more information about us*, it said, in big looping fountain pen letters, *so I'm enclosing our prospectus along with your husband's Documentation of Vitrification. Just in case you might be thinking of becoming a member.*

"The nerve of them!" she said to her mother. "Can you believe it? It's such . . . It's just so . . ." Her mother watched her patiently while Jane tried to find the words to express the particular quality of outrage she was feeling. "It's so *rude*," she said at last, though that wasn't sufficient at all. Her mother gave her a hug, which Jane tolerated, though she was getting very tired of people hugging her when she was angry—did people hug cobras in their flaring hoods, or porcupines in their coats of rigid spines?—as if anybody could be huggable in this habit of furious sadness she had never known existed until she had put it on. Her mother put the unread brochure into the recycling and the DVD in the trash, then made a show of washing her hands before she went back to planning dinner, fussing over the menu before deciding to make chicken tonight and wait till tomorrow for the roast beef.

Jane came back for the brochure and the DVD late that night, after staring for an hour at her phone, lying in the dark reading all the news in the world she couldn't care about, pausing intermittently to look at Brian's number in her Recents—she wouldn't do him the honor of making him an actual Contact—but resisting the compulsion to call and shout at him.

At the kitchen table, she set the DVD aside and studied the brochure's cover, a photograph of the Polaris Pyramid, made entirely of glass. Surely that was the last thing they should make their headquarters out of, if Polaris really was trying to keep things cold in there, but of course if they were actually making Soylent Green out of their clients, then why not store them all in a giant greenhouse? When she'd glanced at the brochure cover earlier that day, the pyramid had registered as roughly the size of a house, but now she noticed that it utterly dwarfed the surrounding palm and oak trees. There weren't any people in the picture, which seemed very strange. Shouldn't they promote themselves like life insurance companies, who always had pictures of happy old couples, or smiling, orphanable children on their brochures, pictures of hostages, really, since they weren't so different from the pictures the Mafia might send you of your own family to say, *Look at how happy and fragile they are! Hope nothing TERRIBLE happens to them!* Except of course Polaris was selling a lie in the form of literal life insurance, and the person who bought that insurance might potentially give hardly a fuck at all for the people they left behind. Why, he might not even tell anyone what he'd done! *Go ahead!* said that person, whose head was always too warm for comfort, always too firmly attached to his body for his own satisfaction. *Let them lose the house! Let them eat food stamps! I don't care. I'm going to the future. I'm going to Oviedo!*

"Oviedo!" Jane said out loud, then added, since her mother wasn't there, "Jesus fucking Christ!" *POLARIS INC.* was printed in obtrusive capital letters at the bottom right-hand corner of the brochure. *OVIEDO, FL.* And then she wanted to go upstairs and wake her mother just so she could say to her, *Could any place on earth sound more godforsaken than Oviedo, Florida?* And her mother might say something like, *Surely mothers love their children in Oviedo, too.*

At the bottom of the pyramid, in a bold, nacreous space font, they'd written *CHOOSE LIFE.*

It was bright daytime on the front cover; on the back it was night, but the pyramid was full of light. Jane opened the brochure to the first page, which was all pearl-white text on a background of a color she now officially recognized and hated: Polaris blue.

POLARIS CRYONICS IS A COMMUNITY OF PEOPLE UNITED IN THE
SCIENCE-BASED BELIEF THAT LIFE CAN BE EXTENDED INDEFINITELY.
THE TECHNOLOGY FOR IMMORTALITY HAS ALREADY BEEN DEVELOPED
IN THE FUTURE. ALL THAT REMAINS IS FOR US TO GET
THERE TOGETHER. FOR OVER THIRTY YEARS WE HAVE
SET THE STANDARD IN CRYONICS, ESTABLISHING THE
BEST PRACTICES AND THE BEST CONDITIONS FOR
THE INDEFINITE PRESERVATION OF HUMAN
INFORMATION. WE BELIEVE THAT THE
PURPOSE OF LIFE IS TO LIVE, AND
THAT EVERY HUMAN BEING HAS
A RIGHT TO LIVE FOREVER.
DEATH IS ONLY A CHOICE,
AND ETERNITY IS
WITHIN OUR
REACH

!

And the facing page said simply:

Welcome to Polaris.
Welcome to Our Tomorrows.
Welcome to Abundant Everlasting Life.

Without reading any more, Jane tore the whole thing in half.

"Oh, Jim," she said. "What did you *do*?"

She knew better than to watch the DVD; she only stared awhile at its soggy wrapper, wet with chicken fat and stuck all over with the leaves from her mother's after-dinner tea. Jane could imagine a whole host of people telling her not to look at it: her mother, of course, who didn't even like an open casket at her funerals, and who would say you ought not to watch something like that until time told you that you absolutely had to, which probably meant never; Maureen would have said it was something akin to operating on your own husband or your child; Dick would say she should watch it only in the company of Jim's friends, and only with a big bowl of celebratory funereal popcorn. Jim himself would have said she ought only to walk into that sort of trauma hand in hand with him. But she didn't listen to any of them, or even to herself. *This is a terrible idea*, she said. She went upstairs with the DVD, the bedroom dark except for the light thrown off by the computer screen. She watched the whole thing once, straight through.

Then she went gliding through the dark house, ostensibly, at first, for a drink of water, though in the bathroom she didn't even reach for the tap but only stared at her shadowed reflection, trying to discern the expression on her face. And she passed into her mother's room and stared down a few moments at the sisters in their beds, listening to them breathe the way every parent listened to their child, in worry or wonder. She wandered up and down the stairs, stepping softly and very quietly, trying not to startle herself by making a noise. Then finally she went down to the basement to look at Jim's amateur sculptor's tools, lingering over the brutal flat chisels, before she came to herself, a little ashamed at how she was deliberately toeing the line of hysteria, when she knew very well she could just take what she had seen to bed with her and hope uneasy sleep would eventually claim it.

She went to the kitchen meaning to get her glass of water and go directly back to bed. But when she turned on the light and saw the head-shaped roast her mother had left defrosting in the sink, Jane dropped her glass and screamed and screamed and screamed. Her mother swept into the kitchen, grabbing a dishtowel and throwing it over the meat in one fluid motion, then gathering Jane in her arms while she said firmly to Millicent, "Get rid of it!" Jane kept screaming while Millicent took the roast and rushed it outside. The floodlights came on in the backyard as she ran out, so Jane could see her clearly through the window as she rushed up to the fence to shotput the meat onto the neighbor's patio. Millicent ran back with her hands over her ears, like she was anticipating an explosion. By the time she returned to the kitchen, Jane had transitioned to sobs.

"How thoughtless of me, to leave something like that for you to find in the sink," her mother said, but Jane didn't want to talk about it. She let her mother guide her around the broken shards on the floor and accepted a new glass of water. In her room, she lay down and closed her eyes. She waited, but of course she couldn't sleep, with Jim's vitrification on a looping display behind her eyes, and with that line from the video narration running around and around in her mind as if drawn behind a plane on a banner: *Next, the cephalon was separated with an osteo-tome and mallet.* Whatever it was they put in him, whatever it was that flushed his cheeks with cold, whatever it was that turned his face to glass, it made him look very much alive and in a state of perfectly horrible agitation.

Brian picked up his phone right away.

"I'm sorry," she said, "I didn't think . . . I assumed this would go to voice mail."

"It's my cell number, Dr. Cotton," he said sleepily. "And I'll answer anytime you call."

"That's ridiculous," she said. It made her even more angry that he had answered. "I was only calling to tell you that I'm going to sue you. It only seemed fair to warn you."

"Yes, I know," he said. "That's all right. Good for you, Dr. Cotton."

"You know? What do you mean you know?"

"It's all right, Dr. Cotton. We understand why you might want to sue. It's perfectly understandable."

"I don't want your understanding. In fact, I want

you to stop using that word. I want you to give me back my husband's head."

"I'm sorry, Dr. Cotton. I know you want us to do that, but you must know by now that we can't. And I celebrate that you want it. I really do. We all do."

"Don't tell me what I want! Do you know what I want? I want to *destroy* you!"

"That's all right, too," he said. "If it will help you, you should try."

"Doesn't that bother you at all?" she asked. "Doesn't it bother you at all that you cut off his head with a chisel?"

"This isn't about me, Dr. Cotton," he said. "All that matters is that you do whatever you need to so you can come to terms with your husband's decision and be at peace with it. Polaris has extensive resources, Dr. Cotton."

"Is that a threat, Mr. Wilson?"

"It's our *guarantee*, Dr. Cotton. I myself am one of those resources, allotted just to help you, to be there for you for as long as it takes." When she didn't reply, he added, with the unclean sympathy of a funeral director, "And you really may find, in the end, that you want to become a member, too. You wouldn't be the first person to follow their spouse into the future, you know."

"You're a *monster*!" she said, and hung up.

She lay there awhile, panting furiously in the dark, but she didn't start crying again. And as angry as she was now, she felt sure she could sleep, because now she had something to do in the morning. No matter how much time, effort, or money it took, she was going to destroy Polaris. It was the first really comforting thought she'd had since Jim died, and she cuddled up with it, imagining, as she settled her face deeper into her pillow, the glass pyramid falling into broken pieces. She had just drifted off when her phone woke her with a ping, to show her a text message from Brian, WE R HERE 4 U, and then a little yellow face, not smiling or frowning or grimacing, but serenely absent of expression. Its eyes were closed, as if it were peacefully asleep.

6

When Jim had stopped crying so hard, he took notice of his hands and feet and the pressure of the sheets against his skin. He could tell by the sharp noise of birdsong and by the quality of the air that a window was open, and he could tell from a soft noise of breathing that he was not alone. He opened his eyes and saw Alice sitting in a wooden chair next to his bed. Now she wore her own pale round freckled face, her features a mix of races he'd never encountered before. She looked like a redheaded Korean, and if he hadn't been so sad he would have laughed in surprise.

"How could I have forgotten my *wife*?" he asked her. Alice only stared at him, smiling slightly. He lay in a very plain bed, in a very plain room, white in the sense of whitewashed, not sterilized or futuristic; a beach cottage room. Sniffing through his dwindling tears, he caught Alice's very particular odor, something like asphalt after a rain. "Are you sure you're not a robot?" he asked her.

"I am not a robot," she said, smiling broadly now. Then she added, "You are also not a robot, in case you were wondering." Jim was putting his hands on his face and in his hair as she spoke. Then he gave himself a punishing hug, squeezing hard as if he might make himself pop.

"How could I forget my wife?" he asked again, trying to imply that he wasn't going to get out of bed, that he wasn't going to step into the real world of the future, until she helped him with this question. "Why did I *do* that with you?"

"Incarnation," she said, as if that explained everything. "You were reinhabiting your connectome."

"My what?" Jim said. "I forgot all about the most important person in my life. And then I cheated on her!" He scratched at his face, but his nails were filed down well behind the tips of his fingers. "I don't do that!"

"It was your way forward. It was your practice of Incarnation. No two methods are ever the same, but there are tendencies, and it is necessary that you find your own. Of course you forgot the most important person in your life. That's precisely who you had to forget, in order to wake, and who you'll have to forget again—and again and again—in order to stay." Jim was still kneading his face, asking himself if it was cheating to fuck someone else if you had somehow temporarily forfeited the memory of your wife. Or was it still cheating if you were dead? A widow, by definition, couldn't cheat. Sex in mourning might be hasty or in bad taste, but it wasn't a breach of faith. So too might the departed be spotless. Except, he told himself, that he wasn't actually dead. Now Alice was leaning against the far wall with her arms folded over her chest. She was scowling at him.

"You *do* understand," she insisted. "You *have* discovered the better problem. Someone else might have spent some large part of *forever* trying to imagine the new world, never even conceiving of a challenge they might master in order to enter it. One reinhabits the connectome by a quantum process. How else would it be? Was it not that way for you, in your other, older life?" After a moment, she added, "Your face is not detachable."

Jim looked at her from between his fingers. "You're telling me that I had to forget her to wake up, and then I had to remember her to wake up again? And now you want me to forget her *again*?"

"Except that, as I say, you were never really asleep. And you will have to forget not only your wife but anyone else to whom you bound yourself in love. You have had to take them back in order to now let them go. You had to remember them on your own, to prepare yourself to *truly* forget them all. We can't do that for you." She sighed, still gently scowling, and crossed the room to take his hands from his face. "It was an early lesson for us, how a client's memories were both generative and destructive to the New Order of Being. When we gave them back, instead of allowing the client to discover them again, in his own time, in his own way—then there was always an *explosion*. But also, when we never returned them, when we never allowed the memories to be discovered—there was an even greater *explosion*." She made an expansive gesture with their hands, and a grumbling noise in her throat.

"Explosion?" Jim asked.

"Indeed," Alice said, snapping her fingers. "Instantaneous Quantum Disintegration. Total Connectome Failure." She paused, as if to give him a chance to consider whether he really wanted to know the gory details.

"Forget Jane? Forget everyone?"

"Exactly."

"But how could I ever do that? Why would I ever want to?"

"Because you can live," she said firmly, but she smiled. "And because you *must*. There's no room for them here. You cannot be attached to your old life and expect that you can begin your new one."

When Jim started crying again, she said, "It is good that you are upset. You are upset because you understand. Love and memory are powerfully elastic. If you do not cut the connecting strands, then they will draw you back into *oblivion*. But you will succeed in this, Jim. You are already on your way!" Now she was crying, too—tears of joy, he supposed, but his were still bitter. She stopped talking for a while. She let him cry himself out. He remembered that very well from his old life, that place you came to briefly, when you'd cried all the tears you had. There had only been a couple times when he'd done that as a grown man, a couple worst things in the world that had happened to him, and always when he came before to that cried-out place it had been a very fatigued sort of peace that he had felt there. But now he wasn't tired at all, and he felt too restless—too curious—to be at peace.

"Did you just say my name?" he asked. "I don't think you ever said my name before."

"Well," she said, wiping her eyes. "I try not to get too attached, before a client Incarnates successfully."

"That's probably smart," he said, and then they were quiet again for a little while. "I'm really here?"

"You are *here*, Jim." She stood up, but didn't offer him her hand. After a pause he lifted his legs and swung them to the floor.

"It's very hard," he said, at the feel of the wood, and he grabbed at the varnish with his toes, appreciating very distinctly the squeaking noises he made. "Should I try to stand?" he asked. She nodded. However long he had been asleep or frozen or suspended or dead, it ought to have been harder to stand up. His first steps ought to have been as halting as a newborn fawn's, but his feet were perfectly confident and his legs were strong.

"Incarnation," she said when he looked at her, making a gesture at him like she was pointing with her whole body. "It is thus."

He put his hands out, as if doing that could help him with a mental unbalance. "Forget them?" he asked again. "Forget everyone? Jane and Millicent and Marilynne? Rudy? The cat?" He closed his eyes in a panic, because it seemed like anything he looked at in the room or in the whole new world would cost him some person or place or thing in the old one, but he opened them as soon as she told him to, and when she pulled him to the white-curtained window he went without much resistance.

"Everyone," she said. "Every last one." Did she have to be so happy about it? Though he was all cried out for the moment, he could feel his well of tears for Jane already filling up again. He wanted to see her face again, but at the same time, he wanted to see what was outside the window.

"I can't remember the name of my cat," he told Alice. "I don't even remember what it looked like. Just when it died. That was in the fall of 2011. Kidney failure. But I forget its name."

"And so we begin," she said, parting the curtains and putting a hand at the small of his back, as if to keep him from turning away.

7

"Only an Ahab should ever sue in anger," her mother told her, standing behind her at the vanity and meticulously shaping Jane's hair into a bun. They were getting ready to go out on their first lawyer visit. "Do you have any idea how long these things take? You don't have that kind of stamina. Nobody does."

"I've got stamina," Jane said, looking past her own reflection into the reaches of the mirror, where she could see Millicent dancing, Jim's oversize headphones on her head and his old iPod in her hands. Millicent would not stop rummaging in his stuff. That was disturbing at first, but soon enough Jane didn't mind it so much, and eventually she came almost to enjoy the sight of her demented aunt playing with all of Jim's orphaned possessions.

Her mother shook her head. "Do you really want to get involved in this sort of thing?"

"I do," Jane said.

"Hmph," her mother said. "Then I suppose I'll just have to be your Starbuck."

"Or you could just be my mother?" Jane said, and she could tell that hurt her mother's feelings, because Millicent stopped dancing, sat down on the bed, and started to cry. "It's perfect," Jane added, touching the bun, remembering Jim's voice, not so long ago, telling her to be nicer to her mother. "It says, *Serious Lawsuit Lady*."

Her mother sat down next to Millicent on the bed and gave her a hug. "What's the matter, dear?" she asked. "Did you want your hair done up as well?"

Brian had texted that morning to ask Jane how she was feeling, and instead of ignoring him Jane had replied, LITIGIOUS. He texted every single morning and called every other afternoon, but after the night of the brisket she rarely replied and spoke to him only once, after buying a digital recorder from a spy store in Midtown. She called him to say she had received the very informative Polaris brochure. Then, with her recorder running, she told him, on the record, that she would sue him, and asked if he had a statement about that.

"Well," Brian said. "I can tell you again that's very normal."

"Is that your way of telling me not to bother? It's normal because it's so common, but it never works?"

"I'm only trying to say that we here at Polaris understand what you're going through, Dr. Cotton."

"That's just absurd, Mr. *Wilson*. That statement is *absurd*. Your company is *absurd*. The work you do is *absurd*. And your name, sir, is *absurd*."

"It's a very common name, Dr. Cotton. And is it

really so absurd to think we might have seen you before, or someone like you, and know from experience how you feel? Don't you ever say that to your patients? *I understand what you're going through*? Or, *I know how you feel*? Because you do meet them again and again, don't you? All those very different people with the same or similar problems? In some way, don't you know what's going to happen to them?"

"How do you know I have patients? How do you even know my job?"

"We know all about you, Dr. Cotton. Of course we know. You're part of the Polaris family, even if you're not a member."

"Did you just say you *know all about me*?"

"We care about you, Dr. Cotton," Brian said. "Because of your husband, for the sake of your husband, we care about you a great deal."

She told the first lawyer, Mr. Jones, that she thought they must be spying on her, and played him the recording of her phone conversation with Brian.

"Well, I'm sure they do know a great deal. The application is incredibly intrusive," the lawyer said. He was a friend of the hospital counsel and had handled a complicated vitrification patent dispute five years before in which Polaris had been a defendant. So he had, in a sense, sued them and won, though Jane knew soon after they started talking that he wasn't going to take her on as a client.

"Look, I know my colleague told you that you're overreacting," Mr. Jones continued. "But I would argue that these people give one no choice. They're too smug. It wouldn't be the first time a plaintiff was caught between *the law is on the other guy's side* and *something simply has to be done.*"

"Then you'll take the case?"

"Oh, no," he said. "I can't. But I think I know someone who might." He wrote a name down and shook Jane's hand and wished her good luck. She walked out feeling vindicated and disappointed at the same time. In the waiting room, her mother looked up from the *Yale Law Review* and asked, "Shall we go home now?"

"For a little while," Jane said. It was a week before she got an appointment with another lawyer in what became a lengthening chain of referrals, but the next one came just a few days after that, and soon enough she was being passed off from one person to the next all in the same day. Within a couple weeks, they had spiraled from the Upper East Side down to Midtown, then up to Queens and finally out to Flatbush before they landed in Scotch Plains, New Jersey, in an office belonging to Mr. Daniel Flanagan, a puffy-faced man with the biggest hands Jane had ever seen. *Strangling hands*, she thought approvingly, probably because he had actually played a murderer on television, which she knew because his waiting room was decorated with the framed stills from the episode.

Wanda, Mr. Flanagan's receptionist and wife, had greeted them and asked them to sit down in the waiting room. The coffee table was full of *Playboy*s and a single black NRSV Bible. Her mother and her aunt each took up something to read, while Jane filled out a short questionnaire about the nature of her problem, then wrote a summary in the space provided on the last page: *My husband's head was taken from his body and frozen by a suspicious company and while it all appears to have been technically legal it is unbearable. Please help me get my husband's head back!*

Jane always studied her patients' questionnaires before she met them, but Mr. Flanagan read hers as she sat in front of him, surrounded by the various diplomas and certificates on his wall. He had been to law school and the police academy and had done a master class with Joan Collins. He was certified as a private investigator by the Colonel of the New Jersey Police, and as a matchmaker by the Matchmaking Institute of Westfield. He had had his picture taken with the last three presidents of the United States.

"Jesus," he murmured as he was reading, then "Jesus Christ!" and finally, after he had finished, "Jesus fucking Christ!" He put down the paper and reached over his desk to take Jane's hand, chasing it and capturing it when she moved it away. "Are you fucking kidding me?" he asked her, very earnestly.

"I am not," she said. Mr. Flanagan now began to pump her hand, as if to congratulate her for her strange tale and her unique problem and her furious anger.

"Wanda!" he said. "Come in here!" When his wife rushed in he gave her a few of the most atrocious salient details.

"Oh, my God!" she said.

"Do you believe this shit?" he asked her. She said she

did not believe it. She sat down next to Jane and took her other hand, and shortly after that called Millicent and Jane's mother in as well. They never actually got around to a discussion of the legal merits of the case, and in fact Jane thought they would have felt a little irrelevant, had they come up. Mr. Flanagan and his wife did nothing but agree with her. They agreed that Jim's body had been *molested*, that Polaris was indeed *sinister* and in fact *disgusting*, that no one should have insult added to injury the way it had been done to her. It was *unfair* and *ridiculous*. It *could not and should not be borne.* Jane started to cry, as much from anger again as from sadness, and Millicent was crying as well. Jane's mother was frowning hard. Wanda was a total mess, and Mr. Flanagan's bald head was almost purple.

"I promise you," he said, even though he had told her five times already that he wasn't going to make any promises, "we'll get him back."

8

There was Sondra from Menlo Park in 1985 and her social worker Alice, and Franklin from Albuquerque in
1992 and his social worker Alice, and Judy from Detroit
in 2035 and she had an Alice, too. Everyone had an Alice,
who were all (Jim's Alice told him) of the same *presence*
but not the same *substance*; they all acted and sounded
like the same person, but no two looked the same. There
was Brenda from Northampton in 2041 and her Alice,
and Eagle from the Wisconsin Freestate Experiment in
2049 and her Alice, and Blanket from the United Islands
of Atlantis in 2067 and her Alice. Folly, a tall black woman,
came from an orbital ring habitat in the year 2085; her
Alice was an albino. And then there was a thin person of
indeterminate sex, who introduced itself to Jim as Ahh!
from Lacus Oblivionis up on the moon, who had glowing multicolored hair and was translated in the year 2101.
Ahh!'s Alice was as sexless as its client. In the evening of
Jim's first day, all his fellow residents in the halfway house
celebrated his arrival with a feast.

"They think they're special," said Sondra, his leftward neighbor at the long farm table, "just because they're from the future. Which could not be more relative. Right?"

"Exactly," said Franklin, on Jim's other side. "They may be from the future, but they're not from the *future*. I bet you a hundred bucks we all get out of this house before they do."

"Is there still such a thing as money?" Jim asked.

"Who knows?" Sondra said, raising her glass as if to make a toast but only glaring at everyone. "We can't know, can we, until we make our Debut. I like that. *Debut*." She made jazz hands at them. "It sounds like the future is one big musical."

Jim noticed his own Alice sitting in a little cluster of social workers, and waved. That morning, she had let him stare out the window until he cried himself out again, and then she said, "It's beautiful, isn't it?" For a moment he thought she meant the pain in his heart, but of course she was talking about the view over the orchard and the creek to a series of rolling wooded hills. "Are we in California?" he asked her.

"No."

"Italy? Tuscany?"

"No."

"Where are we?"

"Let's go for a walk," she said. She drew him out of the bedroom, pointing out his bathroom as they passed it and telling him she'd teach him how to use the fixtures later. She walked him through the house, identifying all the rooms, which she called not by their function but in association with some person she said loved it best. "And this one is Judy's favorite," she said in a little solarium upstairs from his room.

"Who's Judy?" he asked. "Who are these people you're talking about?"

"Your crèchemates, of course," she said. "Now there are nine of you. We learned that, too, that loneliness delayed or diminished the Debut. So we bring you out in clusters, for fellowship and for love, until your time here in the house is over."

"Oh, I see," Jim said calmly, though the thought of other people in the house made him want to start crying again. It was a few more rooms before he could ask, without his voice breaking, where they all were.

"Camping!" Alice said. "But they'll return soon." They were in the kitchen, Sondra's favorite room, which opened directly onto the terrace. As Alice took him into the open air, Jim wondered if he was dressed properly to go outside—loose white silk pants and a sleeveless shirt—or if this was just what men wore in the future, Don Johnson pajamas, while the women all dressed like sexy nurses. Alice was patient when he slowed down and stepped cautiously on the terra-cotta tiles of the terrace. They were warm underneath his feet.

"Can I ask you . . ." Jim started to say, but she shushed him. They were entering the orchard—it was apple or pear trees or both. He couldn't tell because the fruit was all so small and young.

"No questions. Just walking and listening. With your ears and your skin. Listen with your *toes*."

"But what if *she's* here?" Jim asked. "It's not too crazy, is it? To think she might have followed me?" When Alice tried to put a finger to his lips he grabbed it and held on tight. "I won't let go of your finger until you answer me." But his hands were sweaty and she popped her finger out easily.

She sighed, then frowned. "If your former wife were in the future," she said, "you would never know it. Not on this side of your Debut. The challenge is the same for all of you, no matter when you lived your first life. The same for woman, man, or other. *If* she were here, the challenge would be the same for her."

"She'd have to forget me?"

Alice made one slow, grave nod.

"But then we might be reunited again, eventually, after the Debut?"

"You are facing the wrong direction," Alice said, grabbing him by his shoulders and turning him irresistibly. "If you are going to speak when you ought to be listening, then you should at least ask questions that can be answered." She gave him a push. "Now *listen*. With your toes!"

"But a person can't listen with their . . ." he began to say, but his toes convinced him otherwise before he could finish his sentence. "Oh!" he said. It wasn't really listening, of course, but his toes were taking information out of the grass that seemed to be more than just tactile. "Oh, that's nice!" he said, going step by step through the orchard. Alice followed. "You will be ready to make your Debut," she murmured behind him, "when you have utterly Examined and emptied yourself of every memory of your past. That is your *only* job while you're here in the house. But it's easier to consider, isn't it, when you are listening with your toes?" They passed through the orchard and over the creek, then went farther, past a barn and through a meadow, up and down a hill and along the edge of a wood, Alice all the while describing what Jim had to do to become not just a visitor in but a *citizen of* the new world. "Incarnation, Examination, Debut. Always in that order. You've got to be empty before you can be filled. And yes, there will be a test here and there, and daily exercises to help you on your way, but we can't really *test* you on this any more than we could *do* it for you. We've learned better than to try to decide for you what part of who you *are* doesn't depend on who you *were* or who you *loved*. Not even our best quantum mind-surgeons would dare ever try to wield such subtle knives. So *you* have to do it. *You* find the memories. *You* make the cuts with a knife that *you* make *yourself*." She was quiet then, though Jim could hear her stepping behind him—he was distracted by his feet and toes, so sensitive now that he barely had room in his head to appreciate anything except how it felt to walk on the damp green moss that covered all the ground beneath the trees.

"Mind surgery?" he asked, turning around. But now he was alone in the woods. "Alice? Hello?" He thought he heard her sigh behind him, but when he turned it was nothing but trees. "Goddamn," he said. They'd been walking only for an hour on the way out, but it took him almost five to get back, and he might never have found his way if he hadn't crossed his own lost wandering path in the woods and been calm or exhausted enough to notice the tingle in his feet when he went where his marvelous new toes had already been. It ought to have been nicer to be alone then, once he knew it was just a matter of time and distance before he came back to the house. But loneliness made the wrong kind of room in his head, inviting anxiety instead of exultation, and nostalgia for all the things he was supposed to remember so he could forget them again. Might he be able to live without Jane, he asked himself, if he couldn't *think* about her all the time? Wasn't that just what happened, when you finally outlived your grief?

Except she might not really be dead. She might be here, challenged like him to forget her old life in order to start a new one. He closed his eyes and leaned against a tree and curled his toes up so he could think about that. They'd started over before. That would be nothing new. They'd started over, for instance, after his accident, though not in the dramatic way Alice was talking about now, what with the total forgetting and the absolute requirement that fate bring them together again, since he and Jane wouldn't know anymore to look for each other. He could almost believe it might happen—just waking up in the future was already proof of the impossible, after all. But he couldn't imagine that Jane wouldn't somehow feel what he'd done, when they met again on the other side of amnesia, or that she could ever forgive him for it.

Always together—he'd promised it, too. Never apart.

Of course they'd both broken that promise over and over, mostly in imaginary ways, the sort of daydream unfaithfulness and desultory withdrawal that Jim thought were necessary to keeping faith. His Polaris contract had been something like that, a way to withdraw from his wife without *actually* withdrawing, a potential withdrawal, a theoretical betrayal. Except now, ages later and yet quite suddenly, it was real.

Eventually, Jim caught a glimpse of the house, and then a whiff of dinner, and felt how hungry he was. And maybe because his ears were as special and as new as his feet, he heard the laughter and clink of glasses long before he got back. There was nothing forced about his big relieved grin when he arrived to see all his new peers and their social workers gathered around the farm table for his welcome feast. When Jim walked in, they cheered. "I'm so proud of you," his Alice said, after they had all introduced themselves, and Jim had bowed at each of them. Then, with a bowl of cool water and a warm towel, Alice washed and dried his feet.

When she went back to her place at the table, Jim took the only other open seat.

"Are you like me?" Sondra asked him when he sat down.

"Like what?" Jim asked.

"Lay off him," said Franklin. "Can't you see he just lost his training wheels?" He passed Jim a glass of wine.

"Like, *old*," said Sondra. "I bet you're from 1970. Am I right?"

"Sort of," Jim said. "In 1970 I was ten years old."

"Lay off," Franklin said again, putting an arm around Jim. "Can't you see he's a newbie-delirious?"

"I'm all right," Jim said, draining his glass and holding it out for Sondra to refill. "I like this wine. I'd kind of like to taste it with my *toes*."

"Ha!" said Franklin. "Just wait till your tongue really kicks in."

"Everything is better here in the future," said Sondra. But she rolled her eyes.

Jim really did like the wine. He really liked the food. He really liked talking to Franklin and Sondra or even just looking at them and all the others, each of them dressed alike but very different-looking, having died at different ages and in different times. *I'm not thinking about anything but right now,* he said silently, not sure, under the influence of the wine, if he was talking to Jane or to Alice.

"Hey," he said to his new friends, lowering his voice. "Tell me about the mind surgery."

"The what?" asked Franklin.

"Mind surgery. My Alice said I was going to have to cut out my own memories. So how do you *do* that?"

Franklin laughed. "Don't worry about it," he said, pouring Jim more wine. "Not on your birthday. You'll figure it out later. We all did. Tonight, you should eat, drink, and be merry."

The others followed Sondra when she raised her glass a final time, and they all took up a cheer for Jim. Then each of them walked over and knocked glasses with him while Franklin stood by to refresh their wine, and Sondra just sat, staring at their housemates as they came and went, not saying a thing, but matching Jim sip for sip. By the time the cake came out she was as drunk as he was.

"I've been waiting for a special friend to come," she said to him, hanging hard on his shoulder.

"Don't worry," said Franklin. "She said that to me, too. She says that to everybody." Sondra flashed Franklin a finger, but Jim didn't pay attention to their argument. He was watching his Alice as she rolled a cake, nine tiers tall, toward the table.

"Happy birthday!" the Alices said, and the others all said it, too. Sondra shouted and sobbed in his ear until Franklin drew her away. Alice pulled Jim up to the cake. "Don't forget to make a wish," she said. The others began to murmur and then sing again, "Welcome, welcome," and even in the humid air, warmed by their collective breath, he could feel the heat of the cake's single candle as a discrete warmth on his face. Jim closed his eyes and made his wish, which was a question directed not at God, who had never really existed for him, but at everyone he had ever loved when he was alive: at his childhood friends and the teachers who had changed his life; his parents and his aunts and uncles; his adult friends and colleagues; the patients he had loved as a doctor and the patients he had loved as a chaplain; and the friends he had never physically met but with whom he felt close in spirit, Bugs Bunny and Batman and Valentine Michael Smith and Billy Pilgrim and Harry Potter, Pope John XXIII and Maya Angelou and Michelle Obama. And then there was Jane, who was, after all, the only person he really needed to ask: *Please, can I stay here and live?*

After they'd eaten the cake, everyone moved outside to continue the party on the patio. Jim didn't join in when others removed their clothes and slipped into the hot tub. He didn't protest when Sondra sat on the edge of his chaise, or when she took his foot in her lap and began to massage his heel. "I like a nice handsome foot," she said.

"My toes are very sensitive," Jim said.

"And I like a nice hairy foot. Joe had feet like a hobbit."

"Who's Joe?"

"Nobody," she said, squeezing too hard. Jim winced.

"Gently," said Jim's Alice, coming up behind the head of Jim's chair and laying a hand upon his shoulder. "Those toes are brand-new sensory organs."

"Sorry," Sondra said, throwing his foot down. She walked away, shedding her clothes on the way to the hot tub, stepping in just as Ahh! was standing up in the water to show everyone her ambiguous genitalia, wet enough now to start swelling up like one of those compacted foam dinosaurs you might put into a child's bath. Jim turned his gaze away to Alice, who was staring at him, as friendly and serene as a sloth. "I think it's past my bedtime," he said to her, and she took him up to his room and tucked him in.

"Welcome, welcome," she said again, kissing Jim's forehead. She paused at the door, which made him feel like a child.

"Such a long day," he said to her before she turned out the light and closed the door, though what he really wanted was to ask if they might not say a prayer together before he went to sleep, a prayer for the dead. Then it felt to him as if he spent the next few hours totally still in his body but restless in his spirit and his mind, trying to find the words for that prayer. How stupid, he thought, that no one ever pitied the dead for *their* grief. The religionists were too busy making the hugely broad assumption that the dead are too distracted by bliss to miss the living, and the atheists all thought oblivion would be enough to comfort anybody who sustained that kind of loss. *Now I am too sad to sleep*, he told himself, wishing that he hadn't retired from the fellowship of the party and the comfort of the wine, and he wished Alice had stayed with him, sitting by his bed and singing him to sleep. But then, as if it had sensed his mood and jumped into the bed to comfort him, the name was suddenly there with him. *Feathers*, he said to himself, just before he fell asleep. *What a weird name for a cat.*

9

Mr. Flanagan had a plan, which he and his wife described to Jane in a series of shouting e-mails over the next two weeks, each message filled with citations of supportive cases, and links to obscure Internet chambers where people murmured against Polaris and cryonics and longevitists and immortalists and futurists and even the very idea of the future itself. Wanda sent Jane frequent (sometimes hourly) supplemental updates on the research. It was Wanda who found the online support group for cryonics widows called the Penelope Project and strongly encouraged Jane to join. *Look*, she wrote, *a group for people just like you.*

Jane had a visit, but didn't stay long. It seemed merely to be a forum for women to congratulate one another on being lonely and depressed. She lurked invisibly for a while in the chat room, waiting for someone to be angry about what had happened to them all, but the five visible members were having only a very measured and passionless conversation about their grief work. When she couldn't stand it anymore, Jane announced herself with a post: POLARIS IS A MONSTER. When the others ignored her, she tried again a few minutes later: POLARIS IS A FUCKING MONSTER!

Clytemnestra111 responded: HEY LANGUAGE POLYXENA3! THIS IS A **SACRED** SPACE!

Jane wrote: SORRY BUT THEY ARE MONSTERS YOU KNOW. DON'T YOU THINK THEY ARE **MONSTERS**?

Clytemnestra replied, BOTTLED-UP SADNESS IS THE ONLY MONSTER, and then the rest of them followed:

Helen22 said: YOU NEVER MIND THEM HONEY.

Iphigenia7 said: THERE'S NOTHING YOU CAN DO ABOUT THEM.

Andromache57 said: THEY'RE JUST A RED HERRING IN YOUR GRIEF WORK.

Cassandra99 said: ANDROMACHE YOU MEAN A MACGUFFIN.

Andromache57 said: **I MEAN A RED HERRING**.

Clytemnestra111 said: THEY'RE A DISTRACTION. WE ALL FLED INTO ANGER AT ONE TIME OR ANOTHER, BUT THAT JUST KEEPS YOU FROM FEELING HOW YOU FEEL.

Jane wrote: I **KNOW** HOW I FEEL.

And Clytemnestra wrote: BUT DO YOU **FEEL** HOW YOU FEEL?

I **HATE** THEM, Jane wrote.

Helen wrote: HONEY, IT SOUNDS LIKE YOU'RE READY FOR SOME GRIEF WORK 101.

I DON'T NEED GRIEF WORK 101, Jane wrote. I NEED MY HUSBAND'S HEAD RETURNED TO ME.

GRIEF WORK IS GOOD WORK, Helen wrote. IT'S NOT

THEM YOU HATE. IT'S YOURSELF. IT'S YOUR OWN GRIEF YOU HATE.

I HATE THEM!!! Jane wrote, practically typing with her fists. AND I HATE YOU TOO. There were a few beats of silence in the room. Jane's cursor was throbbing.

THEY ALWAYS LASH OUT IN THE BEGINNING, Clytemnestra wrote.

AMEN, wrote Helen.

JUST GIVE HER SOME TIME, wrote Cassandra. I WAS LIKE THAT AT FIRST. WASN'T I LIKE THAT?

YOU WERE TOTALLY LIKE THAT, wrote Andromache, and Jane wrote, I'M STILL HERE. But they wouldn't talk to her anymore, only about her, and before long the conversation had settled back onto its original course, which was concerned only with holding fragile memories and cherishing lost moments and traveling metaphorically back in time to put all those shared moments that were your life together to rest like babies. YOU MEAN PUT THEM DOWN LIKE SICK CATS? Jane wrote, and then OR SMOTHER THEM LIKE BABIES? and finally OR SET THEM ADRIFT LIKE ELDERLY ESKIMOS? Then she got locked out of the chat room because too many of the members had sent her a frown.

Mr. Flanagan wrote several times a day about his evolving legal plan, which Jane ever only partially understood. He told her that she didn't have to concern herself with the three organizations who might be willing to file briefs of amicus curiae, or whether he could apply her suit as a mass action even if no one else joined her in her complaints, or whether Polaris, in as little as six months, could be served with a double-inverse injunction preventing them from freezing new heads, at which point he would have them just where he wanted them, and then he and Jane, and every other wife or husband or mother or father or sister or brother or lover or very close friend who had lost some beloved body to their gruesome experimentations, could start to really make them *pay*.

All Jane had to do, he told her, was stay connected to her anger and grief, which meant remaining acutely aware of how Polaris was *ruining her life*, and *interfering with the natural course of her grieving*, and *causing her mental suffering*. In doing that, she would generate the soul of their case, and so her mantra, until their day came in court, must now be *Document, document, document.* Wanda gave her a journal—not a book but a secure Web address with a word processing app featuring a triply redundant save feature that printed Jane's entries automatically every morning in Flanagan's office. Wanda locked the pages in a fireproof safe, and though she said she wouldn't read them, she did. " 'Always together,' " Wanda quoted breathlessly, the first time she called to tell Jane she wasn't meeting her quota of journal entries. " 'Never apart.' That's lovely. That's mental anguish! We are going to destroy the jury with this."

"It's just our vows," Jane said. "What we promised. The promise he broke."

"You mean *what they took away*," Wanda said. "What they did. I'm not saying they murdered your marriage, but it's almost that bad. It's negligent marriage homicide.

It's heartslaughter. So this is great, honey. You're doing great. We just need more, more, more!"

Her husband added that they needed mountains of hard subjective data that would overwhelm the judge and jury, leaving them no choice but to find in Jane's favor. To that end he gave Jane a button she was supposed to push at any time of the day or night when she felt mental hardship on account of Polaris taking Jim's head away and freezing it and refusing to give it back to her. The button talked to a base station in the foyer, which talked through the phone lines to a computer in Flanagan's office, which kept an endless virtual ticker tape of data points like a heart monitor. At first Jane just held it down rigidly for hours at a time, which prompted a call from Wanda to say she was confusing the computer. She praised Jane for recording her constant mental anguish, and recommended that Jane instead just push the button as fast as she could. Jane called back when both her thumbs were exhausted and sore. Flanagan got on the phone to say a repetitive motion injury would only help their case.

Almost three weeks after their first meeting, just as Jane was thinking seriously about going back to work, and trying to figure out where to keep a mental anguish receiver at the hospital so it would be in range of the button, Flanagan asked to meet again. "I'm on to something," he told her, "but I think we should talk about it face to face." She could feel him winking through the phone. "It's *big*. It's enough to make you push the *other* button. The good button, if you know what I mean."

"The happy button?"

"The 'we're going to win' button," he said. "Sleep well tonight. And don't talk to what's-his-face!" He ended all their conversations that way, though Jane didn't need to be reminded not to call Brian after Flanagan had told her even one more word to him might compromise their case. Brian—or some Polaris autobot—texted every morning, but she never replied, and she never answered her phone, or listened to the messages, when Brian called every evening just after dinnertime.

Wanda's diary website was down when Jane went to make an entry before bed, and it was still down when she woke up. The mental anguish receiver was beeping sharply, at three-minute intervals, like a smoke detector asking for new batteries, but it was plugged firmly into the wall. Even the button itself somehow felt less springy.

When Jane arrived at the strip mall, Flanagan's office was empty, not just of people but of every bit of furniture. She walked outside and stood by the door, making sure of where she was—same dollar store, same threading salon, but now the office was just a blank window. She went inside the salon and asked what happened to Mr. Flanagan. The proprietress raised a hand to her face and blew quickly and harshly across her open palm. "He blew away?" Jane asked, but the lady just shrugged. Jane went back to the office and stood in the empty waiting room, calling every number she had for Mr. Flanagan. None of them were in service. Then she called Brian, who had sent her his customary text that morning: WE ARE ALL ALWAYS THINKING OF YOU HERE AT POLARIS.

"What did you do?" she asked as soon as he picked up. "What did you *do*?"

"Dr. Cotton," he said. "How are you feeling?"

"You bastard," she said. "What did you people do to my *lawyer*?"

"We didn't do anything. Dr. Cotton, I don't know what you're talking about. Did something happen to Mr. Flanagan?"

She held a pose for a few moments, one she struck a few times a year at the hospital, holding the phone against her chest with one hand while the other pinched the bridge of her nose, trying to contain herself, but nonetheless she shrieked her reply, imagining Brian was there in the room with her and holding the phone away from her at the distance of his hated, unknown face. "If you didn't do anything, *then how do you know his name?*" Then she threw her phone across the office, and when it wasn't broken yet, when Brian's teddy bear voice was still mumbling sympathetically into the appalling emptiness of the rooms, she threw it again, and then one more time, until it shattered.

10

The morning after his birthday party, Jim showed up early at Alice's door, ready to learn how to evoke, contain, and forget the memories that were keeping him from starting his new life in the future. He planned on starting small—maybe with Feathers the cat.

"You must free yourself in your own way," Alice said gently, when Jim made it clear to her that he thought they were supposed to have a lesson that morning. "They are *your* memories. It was *your* life. It will be *your* new life that begins when you are ready. So it must be *your* work—your art—that holds and abolishes the memories in your way."

"But I don't understand," Jim said.

"Yes, you do," she said, and closed her door—gently but firmly—in his face. When he knocked again she didn't open it, but called out that he might go see how the other clients did their work, instead of asking her questions she couldn't answer for him.

"Why didn't I think of that?" Jim asked, and Alice

answered through the door that he wasn't trying hard enough. He found each of his housemates hard at work in one way or another, and all of them were polite if not quite helpful to him. It wasn't long before he started to feel like he had going up and down in the hospital when he visited patients as a chaplain, a not-quite-welcome visitor who asked quiet questions about people's processes. *There's one*, he thought to himself, considering the memory, the hospital smell and the noise of his shoes on the linoleum, and the way the sanitizing hand gel felt when he squirted his hands before he knocked on a door. But he didn't do anything with that memory but put it aside, which was not at all the same as forgetting it.

He went to see Brenda in her pottery studio (where, she told him, she was throwing vessels that would not just contain but *be* the memories of her old life—she fired and glazed the vessels with great care, only to smash them against the wall as soon as they had cooled) and Blanket in her *salon de danse*, where she said she was *choreographing her lived experience of the old world* (her memories were contained in still poses and then destroyed in violent leaps and rolls and kicks). Jim visited Eagle among a mess of little wooden Jenga pieces, which she painstakingly assembled into tall arches held together by gravity alone and meant to perfectly represent one episode from her old life; when the arch collapsed, the memory troubled her no more. Folly appeared to be training plump black ants to battle one another to the death inside a neatly raked Zen sandpit (she wouldn't speak to Jim, but by her gestures she made it clear enough that they somehow were managing to cancel her memories out), and Ahh!, with whom he spent barely any time, appeared to be very intently masturbating, her LED hair changing color in a panting cadence in her shadowed room. She took absolutely no notice of him, but he imagined she might be pursuing a perfectly representative and destructive orgasm.

"I like that one," Jim said to Franklin, the next to last person he visited. "Because it seems *respectful* to them, you know. To the people and the memories. Like, that extraordinary attention is a way of acknowledging how much they're worth to you. I can't believe I'm saying this."

"But I know just what you mean. And I understand. You have to be *good* to them, somehow. You have to be trying really hard to represent them. Because they're worth it, of course. But also, if you didn't try hard enough, there might be something . . . left over. Which can be very bad for you."

"An explosion, right?" Jim said. "Alice said something about that." Franklin nodded without looking up from his drawing. He had Jim working on a drawing of his own. "You're the best at teaching this, you know. By far."

"Only because I had a hard time with it, too, in the beginning. Who wouldn't?" He had given Jim a large pad of newsprint and a piece of charcoal, then showed him how to draw a circle from the shoulder, and said he should draw a thousand of them before lunch. "I came to drawing by watching another client breaking horses," Franklin said. "Noticing how those horse muscles contain the uncontainable. And what I saw her doing with them was just . . . a recognition, you know? She was going after a feeling—what a wild life she must have had, to need those beasts to represent it! She was putting her feelings about her old life into those horses, and breaking her feelings. You break enough feelings and you're new again. Right?"

"But then you have to live without feelings?"

"Don't be silly," Franklin said. "Then you've got room for new feelings. About new things. In a *new life*. Then you're ready for your Debut." He stepped back from his drawing, a young girl with dark eyes and long hair parted in the middle. "Anyway. You picked a good time to visit my studio. This one's almost done."

"She's lovely," Jim said. "Very lifelike. Did you draw in your other life?"

Franklin shrugged. "I don't remember," he said, winking. "Not *anymore*." He took the drawing up in his hands. "It's my cousin Sylvia. I mean it's her and it's how I *feel* about her. She wasn't actually so special. Some people save the hardest goodbyes for last, but I'm just dealing with outliers at this point. Ready?"

"Sure," Jim said. He put down his charcoal.

"So, like I said: Step one, illustration and integration." He waved the picture. "Step two, consideration, recognition." He gave it a long hard look. Then he shouted, "Step three!" and tore the lovely picture in half again and again. When the pieces were too small to rip all together he worried them individually with his teeth, and growled over them. By the time he was done, the pieces were everywhere on the floor and Jim was backed up against a wall. "You know," Franklin said, when he'd caught his breath, "I think I'm about ready for my masterpiece." He was smiling and his lips were as black as a dog's.

"What's that?" Jim asked. "Who's it going to be?"

"Oh, just some dude," Franklin said. "Now it's your turn." He stood over Jim's shoulder while Jim finished the cat, and he really was a good teacher, asking Jim all the right questions to help him remember how the cat looked, and to put names to the feelings the cat evoked. Jim managed to draw something much prettier and lifelike (and therefore more representative and cleansing, Franklin said) than the stick figure he would have done on his own. *There you are,* Jim said to it. *You were a good cat. We had some good times together, I'm sure. But now I'm going someplace where pets are not allowed.*

"Now hold the name in your mind," Franklin said, "and tear that fucker to shreds." Jim did as he was told. He sang the name in his head—*Feathers!*—and tore the picture to shreds. "There you go," Franklin said. "Now isn't that better?"

"Maybe," Jim said. "But I still remember the cat—even better than before, actually. Now I can *see* it."

"Well, sure," Franklin replied, a little crossly. "You still need to find your own way. That's why I'm not a horse trainer. Only you can truly free yourself from the bondage of the past."

"Yeah, that Frank is intense!" Sondra said. Jim went to see her when he was done with Franklin. Her studio was actually the whole garden. She gave him a hand weeder. "But it's hard, obviously. Figuring out your new job. I'm a lot more mellow than Frank, you can probably tell."

A lot more sad, anyway, Jim wanted to say. That was the sort of bold conversational risk he used to take routinely as a chaplain, but it didn't seem appropriate here— he was supposed to be learning from these people, not trying to counsel them. Still, in a professional way, his heart went out to her. "Too bad they don't need any humanist atheist chaplains in the future," he said. "I know how to do *that*." She took him to a row of carrots, where they knelt together and began to weed.

"Or hairdressers," she said.

"Oh, is that what you did?"

"We owned a few salons," she said. "Well, scads and scads of salons, actually. You don't buy a ticket to the future with tips!"

"I suppose we shouldn't be talking about this," Jim said. "Our old jobs in our old lives. You should tell me about the work you're doing right here and now."

"Sure," Sondra said. "But fuck it. Why don't you meet me later in my room? I'll make you look like Sandy Duncan and you can pray for my soul."

"I don't believe in souls," Jim said.

"Ha! Then you can pray for my *connectome*."

"You can *style* my connectome," said Jim. Sondra slapped her thigh with her little shovel and laughed. When he'd gotten every weed within reach, he started to make the soil neat and flat around the tender little carrot tops. "So tell me about your method."

"Well," she said. "It's simple, really. Which is what makes it so beautiful. I treat each seed like a memory. Or I treat each memory like a seed. Anyhow, I bury them in the earth. End of story."

"I see," Jim said. "And what about the feelings that go with the memories?" They moved down the garden row and knelt again.

"Bury them, too," she said. "They're, like, the fertilizer."

"I see. But what happens when the plants come up? What's the part that breaks the memory? What's the part that makes it go away?"

"Fuck if I know!" Sondra said. She sat back on her heels, took off her hat, and hit him with it. "Haha!" she said, smiling, but he thought she looked panicked around her eyes. "I'm just gardening because I like it, actually. There's no fancy plan."

"Oh," Jim said. "That's . . . allowed?"

"I suppose it must be. Nobody's given me any shit yet. I'll come up with something. What's the hurry?" She moved closer to him until their hips were touching. Then they weeded awhile in silence, until she said she had psyched herself up enough to plant some parsnips. She insisted on spitting the seeds into the little holes, so Jim did that, too, and he stayed with her until the air started to cool and the sun was going down. He liked the dirt on his hands, and the pressure of Sondra's shoulder and hip against his own, and he liked not thinking, for a little while, about who or what or whether he was going to forget. Which was probably why she asked, after another long spell of quiet, "Are you like me?"

"Maybe," Jim said. "Probably. Do you mean tired?"

"Square peg," she said. "You know, no-fitty."

Jim squinted at her.

"I mean," she said, "do you think it could possibly be worth it?"

"What?" Jim asked, though he knew just what she was talking about.

"*Forgetting* them," she said softly.

He took her dirty hand with his own, thinking of all the wrong things he could say to her. *Don't you think your husband would want you to live? Wouldn't he want you to get on with your life?* Those were the things you could never say to someone who is grieving. You could only notice for them when they finally start saying such things to themselves. "I think we have to make it worth it," he said to her. She took her hand away.

"Yeah. Well, I asked Alice for my money back, you know. Me and Joe, we were supposed to come together. And Polaris—old Polaris, 1982 Polaris—they said that we could. He said he'd be right behind me, the last time we said goodbye, though he was healthy as a horse. That didn't matter, anyway. If he outlived me by thirty years, he'd still be here now. But you know what Alice told me when I asked where he was?"

"I know," Jim said. "You still have to forget. It's hard.

It's so hard. But maybe you'll meet again on the other side. Even not remembering."

"What's the use of being together," she asked, "if you can't enjoy it?" She snorted. "Anyway. I just want my money back. But you know what Alice said to that? 'Money hasn't existed for quite a while now.'"

Jim stayed with Sondra a little longer, not saying anything else, just trying to comfort her with his presence. But the truth was she was making him very sad, and also making him want to get to his own work before he felt too sad to start it. He told her it was becoming too dark for him to see what he was doing. "That's okay," she said. "I can do this with my eyes closed. I'll see you at dinner."

Jim went up to his room and lay down on his bed. Sondra had helped him in one way at least: exposure to her sad nostalgia had fertilized wistful memories of his own, and now he could feel them starting to grow, pressing against his awareness, demanding to be examined. It would have been so much nicer to just go to sleep, but instead of doing that he kept very still in his mind. Then when he felt a little prepared for it, he began to survey them, rejecting almost every memory as too precious and therefore too hard to start with.

Stories, he decided. That's what he would do. He'd put the memories into stories, and when he recognized the person, place, or thing of the memory, when he *felt* it, he would end the story and the memory at once. Jane's mother presented herself right away as his first subject, and though he very swiftly arranged a fatal car accident for her in his imagination, he was unable to let her get in the vehicle. Jane he rejected out of hand—surely she would come last in this process. He also pushed aside a whole host of unpleasant memories: his mother's horrible death, his own accident, the babies he and Jane had tried to have and the one that they very nearly did have. Even though he'd already learned a style of happiness, in his old life that involved keeping things like this always half-forgotten. Starting with the babies felt like the wrong kind of practice. So he came back eventually to the cat.

It was just a cat, after all. And he was only lying in bed, after all. He would tell himself a story in which the cat—the whole cat, the idea and the substance of it, what the cat had been for him and who he had tried to be for the cat—was perfectly represented, or as close as he could manage, and then perfectly eliminated. *Once upon a time,* he told himself, *there was a cat named Feathers. "What a strange name for a cat!" people said, whenever she introduced herself, which hurt Feathers's feelings very much.*

When he was done, when the cat was strangled, when he could feel the horrible dead weight of it in the exquisitely sensitive hands of his story, he cried himself to sleep, acutely aware that this was a worse pain than anything he had known yet here in the future. But when the bell rang for dinner, he woke refreshed, and he felt a little better, not about the cat (what cat?), but about everything else.

11

"I had a bad feeling about that man," her mother said, by way of comfort for the dead lawsuit. Jane had gone right upstairs and gotten into bed with her clothes on when she came home from Flanagan's office. Her mother was standing in her bedroom door.

"Who are these people?" Jane asked. "That they could do something like this?"

"You're making some very broad assumptions," her mother said.

"Well, he didn't just go on vacation, did he?"

Her mother shrugged. "Maybe he's fleeing his creditors, or the ABA. He's probably in Tahiti with Wanda, if that was even really her name, counting your money on the beach."

"Mother, he never even charged me anything."

"New Jersey has been full of derelicts and thieves for decades," her mother continued. But then she sighed hugely. "Darling, what can I *do* for you?" Jane asked her to bring the computer and a glass of wine.

Jane went back to the Penelope Project. LISTEN TO ME! she shouted. THEY KILLED MY LAWYER! But the conversation scrolled on serenely, so she wrote, STOP TALKING ABOUT TEA! WE ARE ALL IN TERRIBLE DANGER!

IN DANGER OF BECOMING SERIOUSLY ANNOYED, wrote Iphigenia7. And Jane got two frowns from Helen22.

WHAT'S WRONG WITH YOU? Jane wrote. I DON'T UNDERSTAND! She got another frown. I DON'T UNDERSTAND YOU STUPID PEOPLE! Then the frowns came in a staccato burst, and Jane found herself recoiling from her computer screen, overwhelmed with the notion of three dozen faces (even the lurking ladies were coming out of hiding to frown at her) crowding one another out of the way to show her their expressions of displeasure. And then she actually started to cry, wishing she could tell Jim that the computer had hurt her feelings, or even just tell her mother that all the other hens were pecking at her like a diseased chicken. After a few minutes the laptop began to chime softly at her, as if in apology. When she raised her head up from her arms she saw that she had ended up one frown short of a lifetime ban, and that someone called Hecuba66 had invited her to a private room to talk. She accepted the invitation and typed, with one finger, HELLO? Hecuba wrote back immediately.

SORRY ABOUT THEM. THEY'RE COWARDS.

REALLY?

OF COURSE. I WAS LISTENING TO EVERYTHING YOU SAID, she wrote. YOU'RE RIGHT, POLARIS IS A FUCKING

MONSTER. ARE THEY APPALLING YOU? ARE THEY TOR-
TURING YOU? DID THEY SEND YOU THE DVD?

THEY TOOK OFF MY HUSBAND'S HEAD WITH A CHISEL.

I KNOW! OF COURSE THEY DID.

AND NOW I'M SO ANGRY ABOUT IT I DON'T KNOW
WHAT TO DO.

OF COURSE YOU ARE! SO AM I, **SEVEN YEARS LATER**.

I GUESS THE GRIEF WORK DIDN'T HELP.

THE ONLY KIND OF GRIEF WORK I WANT TO DO IS THE
ONE WHERE SOMEBODY STANDS ON BRIAN WILSON'S
HEAD WHILE I KICK HIM IN THE FACE.

BRIAN! DID HE CALL YOU TOO?

HE STILL CALLS ME EVERY YEAR—EVERY YEAR ON
THE **ANNIVERSARY**.

I'M SO SORRY, Jane wrote. THAT SOUNDS LIKE
TORTURE.

IT IS TORTURE. BUT DON'T BE SORRY. SORRY'S NOT
GOING TO GET ANY HUSBANDS BACK. JUST BE ANGRY.

HOW LONG DID YOU FIGHT THEM?

OVER ALBERT? YEARS AND YEARS. I'M STILL FIGHTING.
EVEN WHEN IT ALL COMES TO NOTHING. THE LAWYER
QUITS, OR DISAPPEARS, OR GETS DISAPPEARED. THE LET-
TERS TO THE DA'S OFFICE ARE NEVER ACKNOWLEDGED,
THE PHONE CALLS NEVER RETURNED. YOUR HUFFINGTON
POST ARTICLE IS SUBJECT TO MYSTERIOUS EDITS AND RE-
DACTIONS, AND WHEN YOU COMPLAIN THEY ALL SAY THE
CHANGES WERE YOUR IDEA, AND THEY SHOW YOU THE
E-MAIL YOU NEVER SENT ASKING FOR THE CHANGES.
NONE OF THAT WORKS—THE ONLY HOPE NOW IS DIRECT

ATTACK. BUT I CAN'T GET INSIDE. NONE OF US CAN. WE'VE TRIED.

INSIDE? OTHERS?

THE REST OF US. WE'RE NOT ALL INCLINED TO JUST SIT HERE AND TAKE IT. SO WE'VE TRIED TO GET INSIDE. INSIDE THE PYRAMID. YOU KNOW, TO DISABLE THE DEWARS. PULL THE PLUG. WE'VE TRIED DRESSING AS CLEANING WOMEN, CLIMBING IN THROUGH VENTS, HIJACKING A DRONE, BUT NONE OF IT WORKS. POLARIS KNOWS OUR NAMES, OUR FACES, OUR FINGERPRINTS. WE'VE BLOWN OUR OWN COVERS. THE ONLY PEOPLE WHO GET IN THE BUILDING ARE THE EMPLOYEES AND THE MEMBERS. THE SHEPHERDS AND THE SHEEP.

THE MEMBERS GO IN? WHEN THEY'RE STILL ALIVE?

YES, THOSE POOR DUMB BEASTS. THE **ORIENTATION** CEREMONY IS DIRECTLY ABOVE THE **FREEZERS**. CAN YOU IMAGINE ANYTHING MORE DISGUSTING?

Jane remembered a family systems workshop Jim had attended two years before, in Orlando. It made her head hurt just to think about it. THEY INVITED ME TO BE A MEMBER, she wrote. SORT OF.

There was a long pause. Jane stared at the cursor.

THEY INVITED YOU?

BRIAN DID. BASICALLY.

There was another pause.

WE HAVE RESOURCES. WE HAVE DETAILS. WE HAVE A PLAN. ALL THAT'S LEFT IS A QUESTION.

WHAT DO YOU MEAN?

THE QUESTION IS: ARE YOU ANGRY ENOUGH TO MAKE THIS WORK?

MAKE WHAT WORK?

ARE YOU ANGRY ENOUGH? DO YOU **REALLY** HATE THEM? IF YOU WANT TO REALLY GET THEM, THEN WE CAN HELP YOU DO IT. WE CAN DO IT TOGETHER. BUT YOU HAVE TO BE ANGRY ENOUGH AT WHAT THEY DID TO YOUR **HUSBAND.** AT WHAT THEY DID TO YOUR **MARRIAGE.** AT WHAT THEY DID TO **ALL OF US. ARE YOU ANGRY ENOUGH? ARE YOU RAGING? ARE YOU FURIOUS?**

Jane tried out one answer: NO, NOT REALLY. I MEAN, PROBABLY ALMOST, BUT WHEN I THINK ABOUT IT VERY CALMLY I UNDERSTAND THAT I'LL MOVE ON FROM THIS ONE DAY. NOBODY CAN LIVE A WHOLE LIFE OBSESSED WITH ONE STUPID DECISION HER HUSBAND MADE. NO-BODY CAN LIVE THEIR WHOLE LIFE IN NIGHTMARE DAYDREAMS OF CHISELS AND FROZEN HEADS AND . . . She stopped because a window told her she had run out of characters, but she already knew she wasn't going to send that.

AND I CAN GET JIM'S HEAD BACK? Jane wrote, when she cleared the text box.

NO, wrote Hecuba. BUT YOU CAN KEEP THEM FROM HAVING IT EITHER.

OKAY, Jane wrote, so acutely aware that she might just close her computer, and change her phone number, and try to forget the Penelopes, and Brian, and Polaris. Or just stop thinking about them. OKAY, she wrote again, and she was writing it for the same reason she would have said it, if she and Hecuba66 had been having a face-to-face conversation sitting cross-legged on her bed, whispering together under a blanket—so she could have

just one more moment to think, and then one more mo‐
ment. Except that what she decided was that there wasn't
anything to decide. She wasn't deciding to do this any
more than you decided to bleed when someone stabbed
you in the heart. OKAY, she wrote. OKAY. TELL ME HOW
THIS IS GOING TO WORK.

12

Jim had gotten into the habit of waking up early to work on his book of stories—there would be one story for every memory he needed to capture and destroy. Some were very short, only a sentence or two. Others were a couple of paragraphs, and a few were ten pages long. But none of them tried to do anything but represent his feelings for a person, place, or thing that had been part of his own life. When a story was done, he flipped the page and started a new one, and he never looked back. He'd been at work on it for almost three weeks, and had no idea what he'd written, since as soon as he finished a story and turned the page, the thing it was about vanished from his mind and his memory. But though he felt lighter somehow when he looked at the fat wad of pages he'd covered already, he also knew how much work he had yet to do. He hoped it would all fit in one book, since he meant to burn it when he got to the city for his Debut.

At 3:30 in the morning, the house was always dark and

still. Jim would creep down to the kitchen for coffee, and then go to his office, a tiny room on the third floor that faced out the front of the house. That morning he had just put his head down at his desk to consider a next line, and fallen asleep, then woke at the noise of the front door shutting. Rushing to the window, he saw Franklin depart the house.

Something in the way that his friend held himself as he walked to the bus kept Jim from shouting out congratulations. Franklin, totally naked, walked very carefully across the lawn—it was a surprise for Jim to see him naked, but it made sense that Franklin would cast off all unnecessary accoutrements before he left the house and even that he would *go naked* into the future. That was all of a piece with Franklin's artistic and dramatic style of mental evolution. Shouting during Franklin's ceremonial walk would have been like clapping at a funeral, so Jim ran back to his desk and made a sign in big block letters: GOOD LUCK, FRIEND! But Franklin didn't look back once on his way to the bus—it had fat puffy tires, and though it rolled all over the lawn, the grass looked untouched where it passed—and once he was inside, the windows were too dark to tell if he was looking back. But Jim tilted the sign from side to side, and opened his mouth as big as a singing Muppet to make soft congratulatory crowd noises, and he kept waving until the bus passed over the roadless hills.

"Something wonderful has happened!" he said to Sondra at breakfast, and showed her the sign he had made. He was intoxicated with happiness for Franklin, though still he ought to have anticipated that Sondra might be sad about it, and so he should have broken the news to her more gently. As soon as she understood, she started to cry.

"I'm just so happy for him," Sondra said, but Jim could tell that was for the benefit of all the other faces around the table. You weren't supposed to cry when somebody moved out of the house, you were supposed to applaud or cheer or propose some variety of toast. So Sondra pushed her tears away with the heels of her hands, and rang her glass with a spoon with all the others in salute to Franklin's achievement.

After breakfast, when she and Jim had gone into the garden to work on their respective projects, Jim sat down next to her where she was kneeling and said, "I'd have to be a very sorry sort of chaplain to believe those were happy tears."

"But you're not a chaplain anymore," Sondra said, not looking up from her rhubarb. "Now you're a *novelist*. Like Jackie Collins."

"Well, not exactly."

"Sure you are," said Sondra, as she stabbed at the rhubarb with her shovel.

Jim moved away a little, and turned his attention again to his book, trying to think about what to write next. A half hour or so passed before he said, "How are you doing over there?" He had been looking over at her intermittently and noticed that she had been still for a while.

She stood up and stretched. "You know, I think it's

time for a nap. How long have we been out here? Six hours?"

"More like one, I think," Jim said.

"Ugh. I'm going to go lie down. What are *you* going to do?" She winked at him.

"I suppose I'll probably lie down, too," he said.

"Well, all righty," Sondra said. "Then I guess I'll see you later."

Jim put his finger on his nose and smiled. He liked her winking, though he had agreed with Franklin that she did it too much—one couldn't be merrily conspiratorial all the time. But they all had tics and gestures that were the habits of their respective times. Jim was still holding his fist out for bumps that would never come. Brenda stuck out her tongue and goggled her eyes in a Maori fright mask to signal her delight with something. Sondra winked because that was what funny ladies did back when she was learning to be a funny lady. He wondered if she would still wink, after she had her Debut, retaining the habit even after she abandoned her memories of Barbra Streisand and Goldie Hawn. He sighed and got back to his work, struggling for another half hour before he decided he ought to take a break and go minister to Sondra. He had written five new pages and felt a little lighter.

Folly saw him in the upstairs hall and smiled knowingly. His late-morning visits to Sondra's room were an open secret in the house. They all assumed Jim and Sondra spent their cloistered time together having sex, and Jim got the impression that everyone found their behavior both admirable, since it reflected a definite commitment to the Exalted Here and the Eternal Now, and quaint, since they could have just been fucking in the hot tub with everybody else.

Fully dressed, Sondra was lying on top of her covers when he knocked. She patted a spot next to her. Jim took off his shoes and lay down.

"So where were we?" she asked.

"Anaheim," he said. "In '76."

"Oh, yes!" she said. "Disneyland on the Bicentennial! Joe was so crabby."

"But he wasn't generally crabby, was he?"

"Oh, no," she said. "He got crabby like other people got colds. A few times a year and mostly in winter. And most of the time I always felt like it had nothing to do with me. Or with us. He'd go in and come out of the mood all by himself. And that time, at Disneyland, he got himself out of the mood with a pair of damned mouse ears. He brought them up to the desk to get monogrammed and then put them on his head and walked out of the store without paying for them. When I asked him why he did it he said he was angry that Nixon got pardoned. I said, 'Joe, that was two years ago, and that was Ford, and you just stole from Walt Disney.' And he said, 'Honey, sometimes the Man is the Man.' What do you think about that?"

"He sounds like a wonderfully complicated person," Jim said.

"He wasn't complicated to me," Sondra said, staring at the ceiling and looking thoughtful. She put an arm across her eyes and sighed. "You know what, darling," she said. "I'm not sure I can get it up today. Why don't you talk for a little while."

"All right," Jim said, though he was really there for Sondra to talk. It was good for her, to elaborate all these memories, even though to anyone else in the house it would look like he was just indulging her nostalgia, since she wasn't *doing* anything to contain the memories, let alone destroy them, and in fact she told some of her stories over and over. They just burbled out of her, and then disappeared for a while from their conversations, until they came burbling out again. It was surely a first step for her, he thought.

For him, it was like getting to be a chaplain again. That was a habit of his old life, he knew, something he wasn't supposed to be holding on to. In fact, he had been forgetting his favorite patients all week long, and he knew it wouldn't be too long before he forgot he had ever been a chaplain at all. But talking with Sondra right now helped him with his own work. It helped him to call up his own memories, to get them ready to go into his book. Often he'd take whatever he'd just told Sondra to his office, and if she asked him the next day to continue the story about (for instance) his grandfather's candy store, Jim would have no idea what she was talking about. But lately, Sondra was mostly interested in hearing about Jane.

He looked up at the ceiling and folded his hands on his belly. "Jane was always *mistaking* her emotions. You know, like a toddler who thinks he's angry when he's actually just terribly sleepy."

"I never had one of those," Sondra said. "A toddler, I mean."

"Me neither," Jim said. "But you know what I mean. She'd think she was anxious when she was actually angry. Or think she was angry when she ought to have been depressed. With most people it's the other way around, you know. Show me a depressed person and I'll show you someone who just needs to go punch somebody in the face."

"I don't think they have depressed people anymore, darling," she said. "Except me. And maybe you. Are you depressed?"

"Just sad," Jim said. "I think it's just how the . . . process makes you feel. You know? The emptying out. That can feel like sadness, but it's not sadness. It's just . . ."

"Eternal desolation?" she said.

Jim almost grinned. But then he got a better hold on himself, and on his pastoral authority. "Anticipation," he said. "Isn't this what they would all want for us? To be happy and free?"

"*They* don't want anything anymore," Sondra said. "They're dead. All that's left is memories. Maybe it would be easier if we could just *betray* them, but it's too late for that, right?" She sighed expansively. "Sorry. I think maybe I just need to try something a little different, you know? Like maybe gardening should just be to make the salad. And for remembering and all that other stuff, for getting rid of it . . . something else."

"Like what?" Jim asked.

"Macramé?" she said. "Lassoing? Who knows?" She

stretched and yawned. "Anyway, all this personal-growth talk is exhausting. Let's just cuddle some, huh?"

"Sure," said Jim, opening up his arm so she could put her head on his shoulder. She nestled against him like a puppy, but just as Jim drifted off to sleep, she said, "I just keep thinking of Jason. You know, Frank's partner. Once upon a time Frank lay right here and talked about him. And now Franklin's gone. And you know what that means?"

No, Jim said innocently. *What does it mean?* But he wasn't actually speaking. He tried hard to clamber up out of drowsiness, but when he woke it was late in the afternoon and he was alone in her room.

Sondra wasn't at tea, or evening calisthenics, which he'd never known her to miss, but Jim didn't start to wonder where she was until dinner. He sat quietly at the table drinking wine and trying to figure out how to introduce Jane into his book—what scene from their life could he finally start with?—but he was increasingly distracted by Sondra's absence. At first he was just a little worried about her, but then he started to feel very strongly that she was not just missing but gone to her Debut. He said as much to Folly, who was sitting nearest to him.

"Then I congratulate her," Folly said stiffly.

Or maybe you're just jealous, Jim wanted to say. But instead he said, "Something wonderful has happened." And Folly said, "Indeed." So that refrain went around the table. But the Alices looked reserved, and his own Alice said that no one had ever left the house for the city in the evening before, and Sondra's Alice only shrugged emphatically when Jim's Alice whispered something to her. When they had all gathered in the great room after dinner, he saw his Alice and Sondra's Alice slipping away and followed them. "But couldn't she just have departed without you noticing?" he asked when he caught up with them.

Sondra's Alice shrugged, and his Alice said it would be very unusual.

Then maybe, he said, she just had a headache. Or maybe she had gone to the city in a unique manner because she was a unique person. And then he said maybe she was gardening at night, and that before they knew it she'd be doing something amazing like gardening on the walls or in the air. But he knew before they got to her room that when he had said something wonderful had happened he had just been too afraid to say that he really had meant *something horrible*, and he was already crying before they knocked open her door, and before they found her alone in her bed, and well before he saw how she'd used an old-fashioned straight razor (and what was one of those even doing in the future?) to cut her own throat down to the bone.

13

Jane, if she made it all the way into the Polaris dewar of dewars, need not actually blow them all up, or sacrifice her own life to reclaim her husband's dignity. There was just a little powder Hecuba called the Kiss. All Jane had to do was puff it into a piece of the cryonics technology, and the rest was all small molecules riding on microscopic winds of chaos, getting in where they didn't belong, thawing heads and, if you believed in that sort of thing, setting captive spirits free. It was Medea666, a university chemist in her offline life, who made it.

Jane didn't say anything to Brian about applying; she just filled out the preliminary forms, which were more a declaration of interest than anything, a few pages of ordinary questions about her background and health that reminded her of hospital credentialing paperwork. Only at the very end was there anything like an essay question: *In 120 characters or fewer, please tell us why you deserve to live forever.*

She might have written, *Because I am terrified of death*. But she wrote, *Because **no one** deserves to die*, which was what Hecuba had told her to write.

NOW WE WAIT, Hecuba said after Jane submitted her preliminary application. IT CAN TAKE UP TO SIX WEEKS TO PROCESS, SO DON'T WORRY ABOUT REJECTION UNTIL THEN. WE USUALLY MAKE IT PAST THIS STAGE. IT'S THE NEXT ONE THAT KILLS US. But that same day Brian sent her a text, just a beaming smiley with his eyes screwed tight with pleasure.

A small box arrived. Inside there was a shiny silver thumb drive, labeled with the blue Polaris pyramid. ARE YOU SURE THIS IS SAFE? Jane asked Hecuba before she inserted the drive. WHAT IF IT'S A TRAP? OR IT SPIES ON US?

THEY'RE FAR TOO ARROGANT TO EVER DOUBT YOUR INTEREST. DO IT.

She plugged the drive into her laptop and when the icon appeared—it was another Polaris pyramid—she opened it. Her computer asked her if she was quite sure she wanted to open the program, because it was from an unrecognized source, and Jane hesitated again, but clicked Yes. Her screen went dark for a moment before it turned Polaris blue. Jane pushed a few buttons in a panic, trying to get her desktop back, but her computer only responded by turning on its fan and making a long trill of high clicks. She stabbed at the escape button, and then pulled the plug, but the computer had a nearly full battery and didn't notice. An animation was starting in the distance of the flat blue field. Jane had just remembered to push the power button when a woman's face suddenly rushed to the foreground.

"Greetings and salutations!" the woman said, smiling as she spoke. "Greetings and salutations!" she said again, then closed her eyes in a long blink. "Please state your full name." Jane hesitated. The woman asked again, so Jane told her.

"Text input!" the woman exclaimed. "Dr. Jane Julia Cotton, Polaris aspirant number 617.460.666, welcome to part two of your application for membership at Polaris. My name is Alice. This is a virtual interview, which should take between fifteen and twenty hours to complete but may be terminated at any time. Shall we begin?" Her blind eyes searched the room for thirty seconds while Jane hesitated. "Shall we begin?" she repeated.

"Sure."

"There are no right or wrong answers," Alice said. "This is merely a process of discernment."

"Are you a robot?" Jane asked.

"I am not a robot," Alice replied, so quickly that Jane was sure everyone must ask that question. "I am a recording algorithm and a speaking face. All decisions regarding membership are made by the Polaris Membership Board, which receives my reports via continuous feed. Please tell me about the animals in your life. Pay special attention to pets, but do not exclude any animal to which you have had a strong positive or negative emotional attachment."

"What has this got to do with the future?"

"All information is relevant to the future," Alice snapped.

SHE'S VERY TESTY, Jane wrote later to Hecuba. BE NICE, Hecuba wrote back. WE NEED YOU TO GET CLOSE TO THE DEWARS. SO YOU HAVE TO BE NICE TO ALL OF THEM! So the next day, when Brian called to leave his customary message, Jane picked up the phone.

"I'm so sorry for my negative tone before," she said to him. "I suppose I took my anger out on you, but really I just miss my husband. I'm sure you understand."

"Of course," Brian said. "Of course I do. And now . . . and now you can . . ." His voice caught in his throat and he began to softly cry.

"I'm sorry," Jane said. "I didn't mean to make you sad."

"Please don't apologize. I'm just so happy to be able to finally help."

"But is it okay that you're talking to me, now that I'm making an application?"

"It's no problem. I'm the director of family services, but I sit on the admissions board, too, and sometimes I wear both hats."

"Did you take Jim's application?" she asked.

"No," he said. "Why do you ask?"

"I'm just trying to understand what he saw in you," she said, too harshly. So she added, "I mean, I think I know, but I want to be sure."

"He saw the future in us," Brian said. "And now—" His voice caught again, but he mastered himself. "And now he's waiting for you."

Jane didn't respond to that. She only said she had better get back to the application, meaning she had to get back to Alice, though as it went on over the next couple of days, it felt to her more like all three of them—Alice, Hecuba, and Brian—were interviewing her at the same time, and when she went to bed at night she found herself muttering to them indiscriminately, in the space between waking and sleep.

At hour eleven of the application, Alice asked, "If you could send a message to the future, what would it be?" Then it was Jane's turn to cry, so she was glad Alice's blind eyes could not discern her tears. Her mind filled with all the things she might say to Jim, if she could believe for a minute that he was alive somewhere on the other side of time. She pondered over an answer, attempting to ignore the desperate accusations and shrill questions that came immediately to mind—*Always together, never apart!* and *What am I supposed to do now?* and *Why? Why? Why?*

"Are you still thinking about the question?" Alice asked, and Jane settled on "I hope you are all very well indeed."

"Do you *really* believe we're going to wake up?" Jane asked Brian. She knew he wanted her to ask that, and that she could ask it as many times as she wanted. It was like asking a Jehovah's Witness whether they *really* believed that Jesus was their personal Savior.

"As certainly as I believe I myself will wake up tomorrow morning."

"But you might die in the night," Jane said.

"If I did, a Polaris team would be at my house five minutes after my heart stopped beating. And then I would sleep just a little longer. It's one of the advantages of living on campus, but we hope that one day everyone in the world will be so close to a doorway."

DOORWAY! Jane wrote to Hecuba. THEY'RE LIVING IN A GRAVEYARD!

IT'S A CULT, Hecuba wrote. OF COURSE THEY SAY THINGS LIKE THAT.

BUT DO YOU THINK IT COULD POSSIBLY BE TRUE?

WHO CARES? NOT ME. I MIGHT ALMOST FORGIVE THEM FOR MUTILATING ALBERT'S BODY, BUT THEY MUTILATED THE VERY IDEA OF MY MARRIAGE, AND FOR THAT I'M GOING TO DESTROY THEM IF IT'S THE LAST THING I DO.

At hour seventeen, Alice asked, "What is the purpose of life?" And Jane thought of all the things she could say that would immediately end her application: *The purpose of life is to not think too much about the future* or *The purpose of life is to do justice to the past* or *The purpose of life is to die one day.* Or even: *That's not really something you ever really know, except temporarily, the answer changes as your life changes* or *That's not something you know in just your head, it's something you figure out, day by day, in relation to one other really important person.* These were all things that Jim had actually said to her, at one time or another. But she knew that none of them could have been what he had said to Polaris. Barely any of it was really amenable to articulation, anyway. "Do you need more time for the question?" Alice asked, and Jane said, "Yes, please."

She couldn't say: *I try not to think about this sort of thing without my husband around*, though that was still the truth. Or even: *Life doesn't have any purpose now that my husband is dead.* Alice asked her a few more times if she needed more time, and Jane pressed her snooze button while she tried out her answers in pencil on the back of a grocery receipt. She wished she had time to message Hecuba, but Alice was starting to seem impatient, the intervals between her repetitions steadily decreasing. So at last Jane went with what seemed like her best answer.

"The purpose of life," she said, "is to live more life." Alice closed her eyes and looked thoughtful for a moment. It couldn't have been more than a minute, but Jane thought it must have been forever, in computer time.

"Dr. Jane Julia Cotton," Alice said, "your application is complete. Congratulations, you are invited for a personal interview on the Polaris campus in Oviedo, Florida, 32788. A Polaris representative will contact you shortly to arrange your appointment. It has been a pleasure conducting your interview. Good luck to you!"

14

Everyone in the house promised Jim they'd come to Sondra's funeral service, though none of them seemed too troubled by her death. "She'd made such progress this time," Sondra's social worker had said, tsking over the corpse.

"Wait, what? This time?" Jim had asked. He'd seen plenty of death in the hospital, but he'd never visited a crime scene. He'd turned away from the horrible gaping wound in Sondra's neck, from the dull glint of bone deep in the cut, and buried his face in his Alice's shoulder.

"This was not her first incarnation," his Alice said, a little sadly.

"Or even her second," said Sondra's. "Though she stayed with us two weeks longer this time."

Alice patted Jim on the head and explained that they would begin the process of waking Sondra again tomorrow. "Don't be sad," she said. "It's not like she's *exploded*. Sondra's connectome endures."

She led Jim out of the room, and the three of them

went back downstairs to break the news to the others. Heads shook but no one shed a tear, and dinner went on as if nothing of particular note had happened. Jim got very drunk, and moved around the table, gathering RSVPs for the funeral service and saying, "Someone has *died*!" To which the reply was always "But not *really*," and eventually Alice asked him, politely but firmly, to stop saying that, and when he didn't stop, she escorted him up to bed.

"But what about the latest part of her?" Jim asked her as she tucked him in. "The part since you woke her up. Isn't that part dead?"

"Well," Alice said thoughtfully, though she looked a little exasperated at the question. "I suppose it is."

"But isn't that *terrible*?" he asked. "Don't you think that's *terrible*?"

"No," she said. "It's not particularly terrible. This iteration of Sondra wished to destroy itself, and now it has got what it wanted. Tomorrow, the iteration of her that wants to live forever will awaken again. What's terrible about that?" Alice's smile was so genuine and unconflicted that Jim wondered for a moment before he fell asleep if it wasn't so terrible, after all. But he woke three hours later, sober and ill, to remind himself that at least the latest iteration of Sondra should have a funeral. He turned on his light and walked softly to his desk. Turning his book over and flipping to the end of it, he spoiled page after page with a funeral sermon for his minimally deceased friend.

The next day was a holiday (which nobody would

hear of canceling): a new client had come to the house in the night. Jim asked stupidly if it was Sondra come back again already, but Alice only shook her head. Still, he sneaked out of his room when the social workers told them all to disappear so the new client could have a tour, but all he saw was a head of short dark hair disappearing down the central staircase, followed by a social worker whom he'd never seen before.

No one volunteered to help with the service. "I like a Viking service best," Jim said to Alice, "and I think Sondra would have, too. Though of course we didn't talk about it. What do you think?"

Alice said the manufacture of loveliness was always to be encouraged, but asked him if he thought a funeral was strictly necessary.

"Yes!" he said crossly. "It really is!" He calmed down as he set up the chairs outside. He supposed he couldn't expect Alice to really understand anything about a funeral. They probably didn't have them anymore, in the future.

He put the chairs in a semicircle, a safe distance from Sondra's bier, then made the punch and cake, and reviewed his sermon. He'd hardly ever presided over a formal funeral, though he'd given dozens of little services in the hospital, rituals tailored on the fly to the needs of the survivors gathered around the late person always (even if they had been dying for weeks or months or years) so suddenly and shockingly dead. The mourners usually seemed to him to be waiting for someone to organize their grief, to close the endlessly strange, eternal moment of death enough for them to escape it, however briefly, and leave the bedside and the body and the hospital behind. Not that everybody needed this done for them, but the people who needed it the most seemed never to know to ask for it.

He laid the hymn he'd chosen down on each chair, weighting each paper with an apple from the orchard so it wouldn't blow away, and he scattered some apples on the bier (not thinking, until much too late, that along with the applewood fuel they would make Sondra, as she burned, smell a little like dinner) and straightened Sondra's robe, and moved the chairs back a bit more, and then everything was ready.

He waited as long as he could stand to before he started. He went inside once to call up the stairs, "Hey, everybody, it's time!" but he didn't go knock on any doors. A few of them, including his Alice, came to their windows to look at the fire once it really got going. "My dear friends," Jim said to the empty chairs, "let us celebrate the life and the memory of an extraordinary human being. Let us celebrate the story of our friend, and hold the meaning of it together, in this moment which we sanctify together in love." He paused.

He didn't ordinarily need notes for a funeral. If he had time, he'd write out an order of service and a sermon, but he didn't ever read them—they always stuck in his head. Now, though, everything he'd written down so carefully the night before was lost to him, even though he'd been careful not to put it in his book, and been careful not to think of it, as he wrote it, as a story to forget.

Nonetheless, that ten-minute story of her life, her fiercely striving, fiercely loving existence, was gone. He could just walk upstairs for his notes and read them aloud, but he didn't want to go inside.

"Well, my friend," he said. "I guess it's time to say goodbye. To this part of you, anyway. I feel that we'll meet again, though you won't know me, will you? Maybe, after my Debut, I'll come back here as a social worker. I wonder if that's allowed? If anybody but an Alice could do it? I think it would be a good idea. You know, like how in halfway houses the counselors were usually junkies, once upon a time. Which is exactly what makes them good at their job." He scooted closer to the bier and took an apple from among the wood, polishing it nervously on his shirt.

"I usually have all sorts of things to say to a dead person," he told Sondra. "You know, 'You will be missed. Your life mattered. I could feel the love your family has for you when I walked into the room.' Half-made-up, of course. But half-true, too. Or true because I believed it, if that makes sense. True for that moment, anyway, because I chose for it to be true, with every death. It's different when everybody else has left the room. When it's just you and the body. I have all these lovely one-liners, but I can't really say them now. I haven't forgotten them all. I just don't know what they mean anymore."

It was the taste of the apple that made him burst into tears. Of course he had cried during funerals all the time, but it was unprofessional to *sob*. He knew he couldn't have looked very dignified, with snot in his mustache and apple bits inside his mouth, but he kept talking anyway. "They should know it, shouldn't they? They should know back home, back then, that we might be sad, too. They should think about how we're holding funerals, too, way out here on the other side of life, for all of them. They should all stop thinking about themselves sometime—it's so *selfish*, isn't it?—and think for a minute about how we're the ones who are actually alone. About how *they* left *us*." He sat and finished his apple, and then he lit the fire.

He added his chair to the flames, and then the other chairs, too, and then as many vegetables as he could pull out of the earth, tossing them from a distance as the fire burned hotter and hotter. It was a shame, then, that the others weren't there, because it would have been nice for everyone to throw a carrot or something on the fire. So he kept an eye on the door into the house, telling himself that his anger toward the others would be undone if just one other person came out to say goodbye to Sondra. Nobody came out, but he could see through the window that they had started to gather in the kitchen. Then, just at the tail end of dusk, a stranger emerged from the orchard, bramble-scratched and sunburned and dehydrated-looking. "Thank goodness for that bonfire!" she said. A tall girl with a pixie haircut, she looked too young and too pretty ever to have died. "I might never have found my way back if I didn't see it! I'm Olivia. You must be one of my crèchemates!" She stuck out her hand.

"I suppose I am," Jim said. "And let me be the first to wish you a happy birthday."

"It kind of *is* my birthday, isn't it? Something smells delicious. Is that dinner?"

"Inside," Jim said. "I think the others are all waiting for you."

"That's awesome," the girl said, still pumping Jim's hand and looking all around at the house and the sky and the orchard and the dwindling fire. "This is *awesome*. Are you coming in, too?"

"Not right now," Jim said. "I have a lot of work to do." When Alice called him to dinner a little later, he said he would come when the fire was out, but when the flames had died to nothing, he went in through a side door and headed straight to his room. There he began to write out all the memories of his wife he had been holding on to in the secret, stupid hope that he would be allowed to carry them along with him into the new world. He quietly and diligently inscribed his love upon the page, pressing firmly as if to pin the words and their feelings to the paper. But since he could still remember what it had been like to want something with his whole heart and know he couldn't have it, he said to himself, *Now it really does feel like being alive again.*

15

Jane was afraid Brian would meet her at the airport. She didn't feel ready to see him. But it was a fizzy young lady who greeted her, holding up a blue Polaris sign with Jane's name on it. When Jane approached, the girl bowed to her with her fists pressed over her heart. Jane clasped her hands over her stomach and bowed back, not sure of what else to do. *Oh, Jim*, she thought to herself. *How could you not tell me you were joining a cult?* "Greetings and salutations!" the girl said. "I'm Poppy."

"What a lovely name," Jane said, pretending to be a nicer version of herself. "I knew a girl named Peony once in grade school. All the boys called her Pee-on-Me, but she didn't care. I never knew how she could be so gracious and strong, but very much later I started to think she was somehow protected by the beauty of her name."

"I wasn't born with it," Poppy said, very brightly of course, as they waited for Jane's bag to come out on the carousel. Jane hadn't dared carry it on with the Kiss inside—Hecuba couldn't guarantee it wouldn't set off alarms at security—and now Jane was anxious that the bag was lost, or being tampered with. "It's my *Polaris* name. It's what I want them to call me in the future. What's yours?"

"I haven't selected it yet," Jane said. "And anyway, that might be premature. I've got one more interview left."

"Oh, the last one's easy! Alice asks you everything that matters. This is just a formality, really." She gave Jane a sly smile. "But it's the most *wonderful formality ever*. Once I saw campus, I never wanted to leave again. I wanted to *go* right away, you know. But of course that was impossible."

"Of course," Jane said, trying to sound sad.

"So I did the next best thing," Poppy said. "I moved in!"

"I'm really looking forward to seeing the campus," Jane said, which was true in its way. She had felt a tremendous pressure of anxiety behind her, building since Alice had congratulated her on becoming a Polaris novitiate and clearing the way for her to take her final interview and become a member. Within a few days Jane had booked her flight, and Hecuba had sent her to an address deep in Crown Heights. Jane rang the bell of an ordinary-looking brownstone and was handed the envelope through the mail slot by a well-manicured lady's hand. She never saw a face.

By her last night at home, the pressure was nearly pushing her out of the house. She said good night to her mother and lay awake with a flavor of insomnia different from the one to which she had grown accustomed in the weeks since Jim had died. She rose every now and then to sniff at the envelope a few times—Hecuba said it was totally harmless to unfrozen, full-bodied human beings. It smelled very strongly of cinnamon and paprika. She spent most of the night quietly dressing in the dark, and gave herself a whole half hour just to sneak down the stairs and out the door. Still, Millicent came down before she'd shut the door, standing like a mad shadow in the dark. Jane put a finger to her lips. Millicent put a finger on the side of her nose. Jane met a cab around the corner with sunrise still two hours away.

"Oviedo is lovely," Jane said in the car, which prompted a snort from Poppy.

"It's a dump," she said. "That's what makes the campus so amazing—you'll be able to see the pyramid in just a minute." And soon enough, as they rose up a highway ramp, Jane saw it glinting above the strip malls. "*Look* at it! We're still three miles away!" Poppy shouted, rolling down the windows, as if to start savoring the air.

"It's quite large!" Jane shouted above the wind.

"Exactly as big as Cheops!" Poppy said, something Jane knew already from the brochure, but it really was something to see it in person, glassy and enormous amid the Oviedo sprawl. After they parked, Poppy led her to a sunny terrace where two other applicants were waiting on a stainless-steel bench, a married couple named Sally and Bill. "Greeting and salutations!" Poppy said to the pair. Sally and Bill did the Polaris bow, but Jane could only wave feebly. Her other hand was in her pocket, to make sure of the envelope. She took her hand away only to dry it when she was worried her sweaty palms would compromise the fine particulate nature of the Kiss. "Are you ready to spend a few hours in the future?" Poppy asked them all when she'd brought them around to the main entrance. Bill said he was born ready. Sally said she was so excited she was going to *explode*. Jane said she might explode, too. The giant glass doors slid open.

She supposed it was amazing in there. She still felt the pressure behind her, blowing her toward the dewars, which made it hard to consider very deeply anything that Poppy was saying. Poppy loaded them onto an electric cart and toured the interior of the daylit portion of the pyramid, which receded upward into balconies and cat-walks. Poppy was talking about membership services and the R&D section and the Foundation initiatives. The upper pyramid was all about bringing the future into the present, she said, while the inverted lower pyramid (the whole building extended as far under the ground as it did up into the sky) was all about sending the present into the future.

"But when will we see the dewars?" Jane asked, when she couldn't stand it anymore. "Those *amazing* dewars," she added, when Poppy looked at her strangely and didn't answer.

"I believe those are last on the tour," Sally said, holding up the itinerary. Jane had wadded her copy in a sweaty fist.

"Don't worry. They're not going anywhere . . . except into the future!" Poppy said. "And I should tell you," she said, lowering her voice, "that Brian likes to quiz folks a little on the Foundation activities. So pay attention to all the details!" Jane felt a little thrill of nausea at Brian's name, and the thought of his actual presence in the building.

"Pay attention?" Bill said. "Poppy, my dear, I've been waiting all my life to hear about this!"

"Can you believe we're going to meet *Brian*?" Sally asked, squeezing Jane's arm.

"It's like a dream come true," Jane replied.

They went toodling along the glass-and-steel runways and catwalks and balconies and causeways, Jane feeling more and more like she was on some combination of very slow roller coaster and living diorama of the future. Futuristically styled, artificial-looking people waved at them from their workstations or work-sponsored recreations, having indoor picnics or doing yoga or playing badminton without a net or racquets. In the future, Poppy told them, Polaris would make Florida the center of the world. Jane, wishing she could say it to Jim, thought very sadly that crazy, ridiculous Florida was already the center of the world.

At last they had gone all the way up, so then they went all the way down, into the basements and sub-basements and sub-sub-basements, lit at first with skylights and then with snaking optic cables that carried actual sunlight from tens of thousands of collecting nodes (Poppy said ecstatically) in the glass walls of the pyramid. The basement was full of research; Poppy told them about a vigorous twenty-five-year-old mouse named Methuselah, which she'd fed from her own hand.

"I think my ears are popping!" said Sally, just as they came to the first of the three dewar chambers.

"Are you ready?" Poppy whispered reverently, as she keyed a code in the tiny door. "Are you really, really ready for this?" They all nodded hard, even Jane, who, despite the pressure behind her back that she thought might push her right through the steel door before Poppy could open it, suddenly didn't feel ready at all. "Then . . . let's go!" Poppy said, and swept them inside.

16

Days or weeks or months later, Jim was ready. He lost track of the hours, and lost track of the others in the house, even his Alice, taking his meals alone and spending the little time when he wasn't working asleep, or walking through the orchard and beyond. The morning he finished his book, he put his head down to rest and was woken again by the noise of the bus in the yard. He went to the window to see who was going to leave today, and stood a long while before Alice knocked on his door and he understood that the bus was waiting for him.

Alice held his hand the whole way to the city. Except for his book, he brought no luggage. Though the bus had no driver, it seemed to know just where it was going, rolling confidently over the hills on its big moon-buggy tires. Neither he nor Alice said anything for the first hour of the trip. Jim stared out the window at the lovely landscape, pretty streams and tidy woods and stark blue lakes that looked like they belonged high in the mountains somewhere.

"Do you feel ready for your Debut?" Alice asked at last, squeezing his hand.

"I think so," Jim said. "I feel ready for *something*. I'm not having stage fright, if that's what you mean. It doesn't sound too hard, anyway. I just burn the book, right? As a pledge. And then I say I'm ready to become a citizen if everybody will have me. I make my testimony, and cross my fingers that they'll all say yes."

"No need to cross your fingers," she said. "You've already done the hard part. I have every expectation that you'll succeed today. You've made this last part just a formality. I'm very proud of you." She pointed out the bus's curved window. "Look, we're nearly there now."

Jim turned his head and saw a slender metal spire rising from one of those displaced tarns. Mercury-silver, the tower looked almost liquid itself. A door opened in the lake and the bus drove in. Shortly, they came to a brightly lit underground garage.

Alice led him out of the bus to a smooth elevator, which seemed to move in a variety of directions. They stepped into an immaculate hallway, so white it was hard to tell the bright lamps in the wall from the wall itself, but carpeted in neatly clipped green grass. He laughed when she brought him into the greenroom, which was green all over, not just the floor carpeted in grass but the walls and even the furniture upholstered with it as well. "It's the greenest greenroom I've ever seen," Jim said. "Now what?"

"Now you can rest, and prepare. You won't see any-one else until you see *everyone* else. But look, a friend has sent you some flowers." They were on the table, a giant bouquet of sunflowers and posies and daisies, all of them shivering, vastly more alive than any flower Jim had ever seen before. There was a card stuck in them, from Franklin. *Break a leg!* it said. Jim smiled, then winced and held his belly where he had a sudden pain.

"Lie down," Alice said when she saw his face, leading him to the verdant couch. "You're pale. It's all right to be nervous."

"I'm not nervous," he said. "It's just a little stomach-ache. I'm fine, really." He closed his eyes for a moment. When he opened them again, Alice was fixing something to his hair.

"A microphone," she said. "The hall is very large. Are you ready?"

"Yes," he said.

"And how is your stomach?"

"I think it was actually my heart," he said. "But it's all better now."

"Excellent," she said, with a beautiful smile. She stood him up and offered him her arm. "Then, James Arthur Cotton, Polaris Member 10.77.89.1, let us proceed to your Debut!"

In no time at all they had passed down a hall, through a door, and up some stairs, into darkness and a noise he recognized as the susurration of an enormous crowd. She took him onto the stage and stood with him behind the curtain. There was a little brazier set up a few feet upstage, and next to that, on a little stand, a large tin of lighter fluid and a box of wooden matches. "I'll be right over there," Alice said, handing him his book just when he realized he had forgotten it in the greenroom. "Good luck, my dear, dear client. Remember, I'm proud of you! How do you feel?"

"Good," Jim said. "I feel good. I feel *ready*." Alice gave him a long, hard hug, and then withdrew. The curtain rose. A spotlight picked him out.

Peering into the audience, all Jim could see was the light on him, but he could hear a great variety of bodies, shuffling and breathing. *People are very patient in the future*, he said to himself as the empty minutes went by without a single catcall. *Maybe because they have so much time*, he thought, and then he began to speak.

"Thank you for having me today," he said. "I'm so glad to be here. I mean, I'm so *grateful*. I really am. It's been really charitable of you all, to take care of me like you have. I thought I should say that, before I get started." He stood up straighter and cleared his throat, and held the book behind his hips with both hands. "My name is James Arthur Cotton. I am Polaris Cryonics Member 10.77.89.1. I am here to formally declare my readiness to enter your world, the world of the future, a world I have diligently prepared myself to understand. I have severed every lingering attachment to my old world, the old life, liberating myself to enter a new one." He held the book up for them all to see, and then he held it tight against his chest.

"By these flames," he said. "I ask you to *let me in*."

He put the book in the brazier and gave it a good soaking with the lighter fluid. His hands were shaking, so he got as much on the floor as on the book. Jim giggled nervously. "I make a mess when I pee, too," he said to his audience. "So I always have to sit down." Nobody laughed, but of course the toilets in the future caught the urine no matter how freely you peed. These people couldn't possibly know what he was talking about. "Somebody used to get angry at me," he added softly. He stood there a moment, until Alice whispered from stage left, "You should light the fire now!"

"Of course!" he said, and he lit a match, but not the fire. "A Viking funeral always was the best kind of funeral," he said, staring at the little flame. "I think I should just say a few words, if that's all right?" He was asking the audience, which remained silent, but Alice was shaking her head vigorously. "Funny to preside at a funeral for somebody you don't know, isn't it? I mean, I don't even remember what's in there anymore." The motion of pointing at the book extinguished the match, so he lit another one. "I forgot everything else, but I still remember what to do at a funeral. You just put your head down and try to bear as humbly as you can your good luck at still being one of the living."

"It's time now to light the fire," Alice said next to him. She had come onstage while he was talking. He blushed. "You can't stop now," she said urgently. "In the middle of things." She lowered her voice. "It's dangerous. People have *exploded* that way."

"I will," Jim said. "In a minute. Just give me a second

to say goodbye. This is what I *do*." He stepped forward and began confidently. "My dear friends," he said. "We are here together to celebrate a life. This man . . ." Alice was gripping his wrist so hard she was hurting him, but he pointed with his free hand at the book. "I mean, this *woman*." But of course that was wrong, too. So he said, "Always together. Never apart."

"Listen to me!" Alice said. "I'm your *social worker*!" She lit a match and stepped toward the brazier.

"You listen to me," he said. "She was my *wife*!" He tried to step in front of Alice, but she bumped him, and the brazier and book tumbled to the floor. Alice dropped her match into the puddle of lighter fluid, and the stage caught fire like it had been waiting forever to burn.

Through the flames, Jim could see the pages of the book unfurling and glowing, the covers spread wide. The ashes rose with the smoke, the plumes twisting into the words and stories and faces. There was something so attractive about the smell. He couldn't help himself; he took a big heaving lungful of the smoke, and it was like sucking all the memories into his lungs. Or maybe they were just unfolding in him, never having been forgotten, only made incredibly small. In any case, he felt very full. And he felt, deep in his burning chest, that he had somehow found a way for both of them to live forever, a way for him to carry her forward with him and forget her at the same time. He opened his mouth to try to explain this good news to Alice as she ushered him away from the flames, but a hideous belch came out of his mouth instead.

"Oh, Jim," she said. "You are *definitely* going to explode." She was weeping now, and didn't seem angry with him anymore.

"Would you stop saying that?" he shouted. *"I am not going to explode!"*

But then he did.

17

Jim came to visit and stood right here, Jane thought, and paused to marvel, despite herself, at the size of the room. A moment later it occurred to her that Jim was there right now. She wanted to turn to Sally and grab her by the strange, harness-like piece of macramé and turquoise jewelry she was wearing, and shake her, and cry, "It's a *tomb!*" *But of course it's a tomb*, she thought. *All pyramids are tombs*. The gigantic room, as big as a warehouse, was sprayed with blue and green light that gathered in long pools separated by columns of deep shadow. The dewars were arranged in neat glinting aisles. It was cool but not cold. Jane had thought she'd be able to see her breath in the air.

"May I give the dewars my blessing?" Sally asked. She'd brought out a set of crystals on a string and was twirling them gently.

"Of course you may," Poppy said. "Though it's probably not strictly *necessary*." She smiled at Jane. "They're down here on the bottom for a reason, behind nine layers of fail-safes that anticipate every kind of disaster that's ever happened on the earth and several that haven't happened yet but just might one day."

"Now I'm asking for *their* blessing," Sally intoned. She had her eyes closed, and her crystal was whizzing. Bill was standing with his arms outstretched to the dewars, smiling and humming. "They're alive!" he whispered, loud as a shout. "I can *feel* them!"

"*Of course* they're alive, silly," said Poppy. "We are *all* alive." She closed her eyes, and seemed to have a little moment of her own.

"May I touch one?" Jane asked, trying to approximate a look of wonder like everyone else was wearing. She found it wasn't hard—dewar-haunted looked a lot like dewar-reverent.

"'Fraid not!" said Poppy. "But you can get *close enough* to touch one." Her smile was bright blue in the funny submarine light. "Go on. I trust you!"

Jane took a breath, and a step toward the dewars, then took off running, as fast as she could, into the stubby chrome forest. "Hey!" Poppy said. "Hey! *That's not okay!*"

YOU NEED TO GET IN DEEP, Hecuba had written. THE KISS NEEDS TO CIRCULATE, AND THE CLOSEST AIR INTAKE IS AT LEAST THIRTY YARDS FROM THE DOOR. DID YOU MEMORIZE THE SCHEMATIC?

YES, Jane had typed. She had pored over it. She had studied it so hard she had dreamed every night since of walking through an endless field of frozen heads, looking for her husband. So there was something familiar about her flight into this forest of silver tree trunks, a

feeling that she had already been doing this forever, or that she would be doing this forever.

I JUST WANT TO SEE HIS FACE, Jane had written. But of course there weren't any windows on the dewars. And though she had followed the path she marked out on the plans (stolen, Hecuba said when she e-mailed them, by a lady from Newark, whose husband had died on their honeymoon), she couldn't know for sure that she was even in Jim's neighborhood of the graveyard, and it was too dark to be certain of the serial numbers on the dewars. But she stopped in front of the one she thought was right, and put her hand on it.

Poppy's shouting already sounded very near, but Jane didn't hurry. She rested her head against the dewar, thinking to herself, *Jim would know what to say.* All she could think of was "Oh, Jim, what did you do?" That came out in a not-very-elegant croak, and then she had nothing else to say, like any other time in their marriage when it was her turn to chase, and his to withdraw like a pouting child, after a fight. And really that's all this was, she told herself. If she could just calm down for a moment and establish the right perspective, then she would see that this was just another awful fight, and it had fallen to her, as it did sometimes, to take the risk of reconciling them.

She brought out the Kiss, asking herself if blowing it all over his dewar, a total discharge of her rage in one furious, shrieking breath, would be exactly the first step of that reconciliation. She opened the envelope and took a great preparatory inhalation.

She held the breath, and held it, even while her eyes filled with tears, the dewars shimmering in front of her. She carefully resealed the envelope and put it back in her pocket, and only then did she exhale, the breath long and quiet, with her head resting on Jim's dewar, and with the very last of it she whispered, "Always together." When Poppy found her at last, she was slumped quietly against the cool metal surface.

"Holy Future!" Poppy shrieked. "What are you *doing*!" She pulled Jane back roughly by her arm, then fluttered around the dewar, checking lights and gauges.

"I don't know what came over me," Jane said.

"Something *horrible*," Poppy said. "That's for sure. I'm taking you to see Brian *right now*."

"Yes," Jane said. "I'm ready to see him now." Poppy marched her back to the door, where Sally and Bill were standing nervously. Jane wanted to bleat at them, but suddenly felt too tired for it. It was a tense, silent ride back up to the ground floor. Poppy put Jane in the front seat, where she could *keep an eye on her*. Sally leaned forward, at one point, to whisper that if Jane had fucked this up for them all she was going to make her very sorry, but Jane was too tired, or just not angry enough anymore, to turn around and tell her to fuck off.

Brian's office was a wide stretch on the second floor with a view through a stand of poplars to the lake. Poppy left her standing at the glass wall, giving her one last long frown before she went. Brian came in and put a hand on her shoulder, squeezing it before she let him turn her around. His large soft beard made his whole face seem soft, and his eyes were in fact as black as the buttons on a teddy bear's face.

"Dr. Cotton," he said at last, but only after Jane had started to cry. "Welcome. Come sit with me." He led her to a conference table and pulled out a chair.

"I have nothing to say to you," she said. Taking the Kiss in its envelope from her pocket, she put it on the table and said, "I only came up here to give you this. It's some kind of poison or whatever. It will shut down your dewars. Thaw your heads. But it's over now. I just wanted to see his face. Or something like that."

"I knew it!" Brian said, pounding the table with one hand and making a kind of wiggly, celebratory motion in the air with the other one. He was just as young as he had sounded—far too young and handsome, she thought, to be caught up in this atrocious business of death, but then she always thought that when she met a young, handsome funeral director or pathologist, one who looked as if he should smell like a sweaty boy instead of formaldehyde and sweet rot. And the beard! It was as soft and curly as she had imagined, identical in texture and length to his hair, so the overall effect, with his plump cheeks and black button eyes, was that he seemed to be peeking at her from behind a bush. He took her hand, catching it again when she pulled away. "I *knew* you would do it," he said.

"Do what?" Jane asked.

"Pass the test," he said, indicating the unopened envelope on the table with his eyes.

"Do you mean to tell me . . ." she began. "Are you

saying that Flanagan, and the chat room, and the Kiss . . . ?"

"It was all a Willy Wonka mindfuck!" Poppy shouted joyfully, suddenly behind her.

"Where did you come from?" Jane asked.

"I've been here the whole time," Poppy said, sitting down now and taking Jane's other hand, so she was captured between them. *"Did you get the plans?"* she asked gravely, then giggled. "It was me. I'm Hecuba." When Jane only stared at her, she said. "Hecuba66!"

"I think she understands, Poppy," Brian said, in his gentle funeral-director voice.

"I don't," Jane said, pulling her hands away and standing up.

"We like to be sure of people, Dr. Cotton," Brian said. "We *have* to be sure of people. And now we are sure of you."

"Sure of what?"

"Sure of your love! Your love of your husband. Your love of life. Your love of *us*. You could have chosen *death*, but you chose otherwise. You chose *life*."

"You must have me mixed up with my husband," Jane said, though she thought it would be wonderful to believe all the things he had always said about life and love and being together forever, since maybe they would all remain true even if only one of them believed them. They'd traded off believing in *them*, after all, hadn't they? She tried very hard to remember. *Always together.* But sometimes it was only one of them doing the work to keep them never apart.

"He loved everybody," she said. "And I love *him*, but everybody else I pretty much hate." Still trying to be angry, all she could manage was to be annoyed by the way Brian was staring so hard at her, and by the way he kept saying her name like he was savoring it in his mouth. "What?" she snapped. "What do you want from me now? Should I just go home, or are you going to press some kind of fake industrial espionage charges on me?"

"Dr. Cotton," he said. "What I'm trying to tell you is that you *are* home." He was staring at her with such total sincerity that she could not pull her eyes away to roll them at him and at Poppy, at Jim, at the whole absurd situation, and the ridiculous pyramid and the ridiculous city and the tasteless trash heap of a state. She couldn't even blink. "Your home is with us because his home is with us. Your home is with your husband. Don't you understand? *You can already be together forever.*" A contract had appeared on the table. He laid his hand across it.

"Really?" she said, beginning to cry, now not only for anger or for grief. "You really believe that?" She reached for Brian's face, and tugged gently on his beard.

"Really," he said, so full of his good news. "Really!" He was weeping also, and Poppy was hyperventilating, and Jane felt suddenly aware of all the other people in the pyramid, on the balconies and coigns of the upper levels, other boys with soft beards, and girls with protractors in their hair, lovers and dreamers and frightened selfish fools. She put her other hand in Brian's beard and held on to his face, knowing, in a way that entirely transcended time, that he had grown the beard so she could shake his face *just like this*. "Brian," she said, and he just kept smiling and crying. "Oh, Brian."

"Dr. Cotton!" he cried out joyfully. "Jane!"

"Oh, Brian." She sighed again. "Poor Brian. You don't understand—none of you do. Don't any of you get it? Don't any of you understand what forever actually *is*?" Then she cast his face away—who knows where she found the strength? Jane cast Brian Wilson at her feet, and Poppy stood frozen when she walked out of the office. She got in the little clown car from the future and started to drive, not sure where she was going, and not sure if she would even be allowed to escape the Polaris campus, let alone this pathetic and ridiculous situation of her life, if they would capture her and forcibly transport her to the future, or have her arrested for her own part in their conspiracy to break her heart. But she didn't care. Really, she didn't. Wherever she was going, whatever was going to happen, this moment alone was enough to hold and sustain her. *Does this thing have a radio?* she tried to ask of the air, because she wanted to make herself laugh, as the great glass doors opened after all and she drove out into the flat Florida glare. But she only said, to the full absence of him, "Jim, I'm coming," and made herself cry harder instead.

18

In darkness, he understood these words: *Greetings and salutations!* Except the words were not exactly spoken, and Jim did not exactly hear them. Once upon a time he had wondered aggressively what it was like to hear voices, and tried to imagine his way into the head of the psychiatry patients who always insisted that the boxes of tissues or the window blinds were piteously weeping and who asked, when he tried to pray with them, why no one ever wanted to minister to the inanimate, who needed and wanted it more than most of the living could ever know or understand. Is this what that's like? he asked himself now, realizing as he asked this one that there were other, more pressing questions to ask. So, in the absence of a mouth and a tongue, in the absence of air, he asked, *Am I alive?*

You have always been alive, he was told. *But now you are awake.*

He remembered, in a very stale and remote way, a great panic at dying, and asking someone—not God, of course—for just a few more minutes, a few more words. He remembered how he had understood in his very body that he wasn't going to get them. Or was the panic about something else? He complained: *My heart hurts.*

Yes. I'm sorry about the (pain). He tried to decide whether he had only been dreaming of pain, or if it was agony to come back to life, or if the pain of dying could not abate if you never actually died, or if he had simply been in some kind of Hell. He supposed it didn't matter.

(Pain)? he asked. And then, after something like intuition, something like memory, *(Pain). (Book). (Funeral). (Alive).* And after that: *(Alive)! (Book)! (Funeral)!* Then: *(Book) (Book) (Funeral) (Funeral) (Alive) (Alive) [Book Funeral Alive] (Alive) (Alive) (Funeral) (Funeral) (Book) (Book).* And finally: *Alice!*

Yes, Jim, she said. *Welcome to Cycle Two.*

Cycle what? Jane! Oh, God!

Cycle Two. It comes after Cycle One.

But I failed. I couldn't do it. I couldn't forget her. How could I do it?

Yet you tried. You tried very well.

I did?

Assuredly.

But that's horrible!

No, it's wonderful. I was, and am, so proud of you.

Incarnation, Examination, Debut—was that all a lie, then?

Not at all. But each is both a local and a universal process. Do you understand?

He did, right away, wishing he didn't. *You do it over and over?*

Yes. Until you (arrive)! Are you ready? Would you like the long answer to the question of how we proceed from here? I believe you are ready for the long answers now. When he didn't respond, she asked again, *Are you ready?*

No.

Very well. We will rest awhile. We could rest for an age, if you wish. There is time.

I mean, Jim asserted, *I'll never be ready.*

But you already are ready.

No. I don't want to be ready. Alice, I don't want to. When she didn't reply, he added, a little desperately, *Don't you understand? I want my life back.*

You mean you want to be alive! she corrected. *You cannot have your life back. That is exactly why it must be forgotten. Do you appreciate how much you have learned? You are already so much more like us!*

But I want my life.

You cannot have it. But you can be (alive)!

Life, Jim repeated, not sure whether he felt like a child or like he was reasoning with a child.

Alive! Polaris Client 10.77.89.1, this is what you wanted! This is what you chose. And then, more gently, she added, *You will be in love again. Do you think no one is in love in the future?*

Who cares about love? Jim replied. *That's the easy part. It's only the first part. We were in life together, Alice. We were in life! And if we aren't together now, then we weren't together then? Do you understand?*

She didn't understand. Then they started to fight, at first only with notions and assertions and words, until

Jim added thrusts of (imagination) to his arguments, so for a few timeless moments he was a pig trying to crush a spider under his little hooves, or an old man hitting his nurse with a pillow. Then Jim was asserting his hips against her hips, or blowing out a match every time she struck one alight. And then for a while she was showing him images of surpassing loveliness, portraits from the future calibrated just to the edge of his ability to recognize them as more beautiful than alien, which Jim answered, again and again, with an image of the dull white bone at the bottom of the wound in Sondra's throat. But eventually all Jim was asserting to her was: *(Life) (Love) (Memory)*. And all she was saying in reply was: *(Alive) (Love) (Alive)*. And at last he overpowered her, or she relented. She put them on a flat green field under a cloudless sky. A hot air balloon was tethered directly behind her.

"Are you really sure?" she asked weakly.

"Yes," Jim said. "Just let me die. Turn it off, whatever it is. I'm ready."

"But I don't understand," she said very sadly. "We do not understand."

"There's another way to be alive," he said. "To have been alive. I barely understand it myself. I don't have time to explain!"

"Then goodbye, Jim Cotton," she said, stepping out of his way. When he had clambered into the basket and turned around, she was part of a crowd of bodies, but her face was the only one that he could see clearly.

"Hurry!" Jim said as she fiddled with the lines. "Hurry up, before I forget!" No one helped Alice with the lines, but they were all waving handkerchiefs and cheering softly at him. "Goodbye!" he said, when he finally began to rise. "Goodbye, everybody!" Then his backward-drifting balloon had entered a cloud, or a wall of snow, or maybe all the handkerchiefs had taken flight to escort him to wherever it was he was going.

"Jane," he said, just before he was nowhere and nothing at all. "Here I come."

CYCLE TWO

1

Jane lay in bed for an hour, not exactly waiting out the dark, though lately she preferred to rise in the light. She'd been getting up in darkness for most of her life, and had never been troubled by a dead stillness in a house, or the quivering gray static she saw when she stared long enough at absolutely nothing in a dark room, but now those things made her feel almost more lonely than she could stand. Her mother, whenever she sensed her awake and abed, encouraged Jane to sit outside on the terrace, so she might witness the remarkable transformations of the dawn and let some light into her *soul*. She never asked Jane if she and Millicent should go back home to Northampton, and Jane never told them to leave. But it was another advantage of waiting for the sun to come up before she got out of bed, that her mother would take Millicent for her long early-morning walk, leaving Jane to herself. They were always gone at least an hour, unless the weather was very bad, since Millicent had to examine every little thing as they went along,

lingering with her eyes over flowers, light posts, and gar-
bage cans the way a dog might linger with its nose.

Jane took her time making her morning tea, staring
awhile at her mother's extensive traveling collection before finally selecting a tiny can of matcha. She had no
plans to become one of those ladies with bitter tea breath
who sits around the house in an oversize cardigan with a
giant mug in her hands, setting her face in thoughtful
poses over the steam, someone who seems to turn tea
into a *companion*. Even if she was wearing one of Jim's
cardigans, and permitted herself to look very thoughtful or sad standing by the kitchen window waiting for
the water to boil, she knew this was an indulgence as
temporary as her withdrawal from work, or her mother's
tenure in her house. She wasn't going to become a *tea
lady*. But for twenty minutes or so, it was nice to pretend
she could actually enjoy a little shallow contemplative
wonder.

She took the water off the flame just before the boil
could really start to roll, having already measured two
precise scoops of bright green powder into a cup with the
long-handled wooden spoon that her mother sometimes
wore in her hair. She poured the water (and lingered,
yes, over the steam), then attacked it with the bamboo
whisk, deliberately restraining herself from picturing a
particular bearded face held still in a vise so she could
attack it with vigorous zigzag scratches.

She drank the second cup down like a shot of liquor,
then got back to work. Alice was there immediately
when Jane clicked her icon (this made Jane think she

must be running always in the background of the computer's OS, watching and listening to everything Jane did, and so she started borrowing her mother's laptop to talk with Hecuba). Alice's eyes darted more slowly this morning, as if she were watching a very sluggish game of Pong.

"Good morning, Dr. Cotton. It's seven thirty-five a.m. on April 7, 2013. Shall we continue your application?"

"Where do you go when I shut the computer?" Jane asked.

"I don't understand your question," Alice said. "Shall we ask for help?" She summoned up a Polaris chat box, but Jane dismissed it.

"No," Jane said. "Would you like some tea?"

"I would not like some tea," Alice said. "Shall we continue your application?"

"By all means," Jane said.

"Very well," Alice said. "Please tell me the story of the worst thing you've ever done."

"Excuse me?"

"Please tell me—" Alice began, but Jane cut her off.

"Why would I tell you something like that?" Jane asked, raising her voice and taking great pains to enunciate. "Why do you need to know that?"

Alice paused, though her eyes kept moving. "I understand your question," she said. "May I refer you to FAQ 217.7 in the Polaris Applicant's Handbook?"

"May you?" Jane asked wearily. "You may." The box appeared next to Alice's chin:

Q: ARE YOU TRYING TO MAKE ME FEEL ASHAMED?
A: OF COURSE NOT. IN THE FUTURE, THERE WON'T
BE ANY SHAME. WE ASK THESE QUESTIONS NOT
BECAUSE WE ARE LOOKING FOR PEOPLE WHO
HAVE NEVER DONE ANYTHING WRONG, BUT BE-
CAUSE WHAT YOU TELL US WILL HELP US KNOW
YOU BETTER. AND WE WANT TO GET TO KNOW YOU
VERY WELL INDEED.

"Oh, Jesus," said Jane. She considered various easy anecdotes—a neglected goldfish, a cruel playground taunt—but suspected Alice would blink away those stand-ins. Polaris already had her husband. They'd already taken away the meaning of her marriage; now—of course!—they wanted everything that was left of it, the secrets and memories that were its substance. *I'll give it to you, all right*, she thought. *Just wait.*

"Shall we begin?" Alice asked, after thirty seconds of silence, and then after thirty more she asked again. "Wait!" Jane said. "I'm thinking!" Then Alice waited two minutes before she asked again, but still that could hardly be time enough to consider an answer, unless you were one of those people who walked around barely able to restrain yourself from telling people how terrible you were, or one of those people who had done so few terrible things in her life she could pick the worst one in a snap. But finally she responded, "Sure. Yes."

"Voice input or keyboard?" said Alice, but Jane had already started typing.

2

She hadn't particularly *meant* to cheat on Jim, but neither was it something that *just happened*. Part of finally figuring out how they were going to make it together was them both committing to tell the other if one of them felt suddenly compelled to try to destroy the marriage. This was almost never a confession of desire for some (essentially random) other person, but a confession of the perverse desire to be fundamentally alone, to withdraw from their shared life, with all its benefits and obligations, to an easier loneliness they each sometimes preferred but neither really wanted.

There was nothing wrong with this. It was, in Jim's annoying chaplain parlance, *allowed*. You might even, as they both sometimes did, announce that you were thinking of taking a *vacation*, and (after some back and forth on the nature and duration of the trip) be wished a *bon voyage*, and then retreat for a few days, or maybe even a week, into a kind of sullen impersonal detachment. That was fine. You just had to let the other person know what you were doing. But this time she didn't tell Jim what she was doing. She barely even let herself know. And so the promise she broke was much bigger than a mere contract of sexual fidelity. And that, Alice, was the worst thing she had ever done.

But Alice didn't need the details. She couldn't possibly comprehend them. Polaris couldn't possibly comprehend them. In fact, Polaris was the very antithesis of those details, which only convinced Jane more and more that Polaris was hiding something from her, that they had tricked Jim into signing up, or that he had signed up with them long before he and Jane had ever met— because he was always better at holding up his side of the bargain than she was at holding up hers. This kind of total withdrawal was something that he simply wouldn't ever do to her.

So she didn't even mention the promise, or the baby funerals. Instead she wrote, *His name was Ben.*

They met in the OR, over a frozen section. Or they might have one day said that was how they met, if she had run away with Ben into a different life, into some kind of temporary happiness that would (she did not doubt) congeal into a permanent and familiar unhappiness, an unhappiness that would look just like the one that had motivated her to cheat in the first place, except it would be worse. Because now she would no longer have Jim to help her manage it. Or because now she wouldn't get to enjoy any longer the sovereign remedy of helping Jim with his own constitutive and situational unhappiness, which sometimes was the only remedy that ever really helped with hers. So running away with Ben was never really an option, though she wrote to Alice as if she had actually been tempted to do it.

It was his eyes, she wrote, though of course it wasn't really his eyes that attracted her. Maureen had actually flirted with him first, but they both had OR crushes on him, and when she came to Jane's office to prove her point about what color Ben's eyes were by googling *cornflower blue*, Jane saved the image on her desktop and let it sit there, one little square among a hundred others. She moved the image around, a marker denoting exactly how important Ben was in the daily sum of her thoughts and feelings—she supposed it reinforced her feelings of control over things, and helped delude her into thinking that there wasn't anything to tell Jim *yet*. But by the time she and Ben were fucking in his office twice a day she'd made the cornflower her wallpaper, and though she sat in front of it for half of every afternoon she barely saw it anymore.

It was Jim and his pathetic baby funerals, she wrote, adding (but only in her head), *He cheated on me first with those grieving almost-mothers*. Of course it wasn't really that, either, but that was what she and Jim talked about, once it was already too late to talk about it. She had sex with Ben for the first time the day after the evening that Jim came home and told her, in excruciating detail, about the service he had performed for a stillborn baby on the tenth floor of the children's hospital. He said it was like *his pain came out of him* to mingle with the pain of the almost-parents. Except that he told them, of course, that they *were* parents. "And when I pronounced them parents," he said of the dead-baby baptism he'd been waiting three years to perform, "for just a second I thought the baby was going to start *crying*."

"That's really great," Jane said, and she cried with him, though she wasn't crying for the reason he thought she was crying.

She never met with Ben outside of the hospital—in the six weeks it lasted, the relationship never progressed that far. But the hospital covered twenty square blocks of Washington Heights, so there were all sorts of places to go and even people to see, if you counted security guards and volunteers and patients as people, since they avoided nurses and other physicians and especially the gossipy chaplains. There were lovers' vistas to enjoy, gorgeous views of the river or the downtown skyline from empty rooms, and twice they even had a sit-down dinner, with real napkins, at the strange little restaurant on the eighth floor, attached to the VIP unit, which had once been patient rooms. "It's like the French Laundry," Ben said, "but with patient smell."

"The French Stroke Unit," Jane said. She wanted to spend the night with him, but they never did that, even though Ben spent the night in his office all the time. He practically lived there—Jane hadn't ever known a pathologist who worked so hard. If he'd had a bed in his office, she might have dared. She spent the night in call rooms all the time, after a long case, or even when she had a little patient whose post-op management she didn't totally trust to the ICU. Jim wouldn't have thought twice about that kind of absence from her. But the nearest she came were the postcoital naps, on a couch that didn't really leave any room to cuddle, so she had to sprawl on top of Ben like a dog. That's when she came closest to asking for what she really wanted, an intimacy more obscene than any sexual experience they pursued. She meant to burst into tears on top of him in the middle of the radically uncomfortable cuddle, so that, without even finding out what was wrong, he could tell her he was sorry, that he loved her, and that everything was always going to be okay in the end.

"I can't believe," he said, in line for a miserable plate of eggs in the hospital cafeteria on their last morning together, "that we've still got the whole morning ahead of us, and then the whole day."

"And then I can come home with you," she said.

"Really?"

"Not really," she said. She put on a show of rudeness for anyone listening or reading her lips, careful to hold herself a certain way when they were together in public. But she was already being mean to him in private as well, as if to punish him for not giving her the thing she wouldn't ask him for. They had worked a case together that morning, so they might just be discussing histology, as far as anyone watching might be concerned.

"Aww," he said, and she flinched because she thought he was going to put his arm around her. "Just getting some ketchup," he said.

"Sorry," she said. She watched his omelet being prepared. The fry cook was staring hard at the eggs, like he was going to punish them with the fistful of cheddar he held, flinging the cheese like pebbles into a face. So she didn't notice when Dick and Jim joined them in line.

"Good morning," said Jim.

"Blessed be!" said Dick.

"Oh, hi," said Ben, blushing like a fool. Jane smiled at her husband, her first impulse being to *act nonchalant*. It was the first time he'd seen her together with Ben, something she'd been avoiding so successfully for weeks. She had feared that if he saw them together he would know right away what was going on.

Her smile was desperate. Jim cocked his head at her inscrutably. She looked away.

"Blessed be!" Dick repeated brightly, and Ben made the sign of the cross at them, smiling and nodding in response.

"I don't believe in God," Jim said flatly. "So that bothers me a little."

"Oh, sorry," Ben said. "Like a vampire, huh?" he added, into the resulting silence.

"Actually, I think most people who think of themselves as vampires do believe in God. It's part of their existential pain. Don't they, Dick?"

"The one I counseled certainly did."

"You counseled a vampire?" asked Ben.

"Well, he *thought* he was a vampire. Which is the same thing, pastorally speaking. He worked in a blood bank and nipped at those little sausagey bits that are attached to the bag."

"They're samples," Ben said. "To test for the cross match."

"They're not enough to live on, you can imagine. But he couldn't bring himself to sip off the bag itself, because of the infection risks—to others, not to himself. And he couldn't bear the thought of drinking a whole bag when someone might *need* it. He was very conscientious. It was just an addiction, of course. Anything can be an addiction, and his was blood. There was something underneath it, of course. A spiritual problem. We worked it out. But that's a longer story. Shall we sit together? I could tell you the whole thing." They had all moved along down the breakfast line.

"Chaplains and doctors sitting together?" Jim said. He'd taken only a piece of toast and a boiled egg. "Dogs and cats will dance in the streets first."

"Haha!" said Ben.

"Sometimes dogs and cats get married," said Jane.

"Actually, I was a surgeon back then," Jim said to Ben. "I wasn't always a chaplain. I took up the chaplain thing after my accident. Too shaky now." He held up a fist between them, and let it tremble freely. "But sometimes it feels like being a doctor, without all the cutting and stuff."

"It sounds amazing," Ben said.

"Indeed," Jim said, " 'Amazing Things Are Happening Here.' " That was the hospital slogan this week, or this month. Jim wasn't sure. Just when he had received "Putting Patients First" fully into his heart, they had gone and changed it. "I'm going to take mine to go. Dick, you staying?"

"Let's have coffee," Dick said to Ben. Jim could feel Jane's gaze burning on him, but he didn't look at her again, not even to say goodbye when he and Dick took their leave and started back across the skybridge to the old hospital and the chaplain offices.

"What was that about?" said Dick. "Couldn't you see it? I had him right where I wanted him. I was about to get an in. That poor man!" Dick had been the chaplain on duty for staff one day when Ben had wandered into the chapel to start an abortive conversation about sex addiction. Ordinarily, Jim would never have heard about it, but Dick had brought it up in peer supervision. Back at the office, Dick picked at his eggs and said, "My heart goes out to him."

"And something else goes out, also engorged with blood."

"Don't be silly," Dick said. "This isn't sexual, it's *pastoral*. What's wrong with you today?"

"Nothing," Jim said. "Sorry."

"It's all right," said Dick. "But let's pray about it, before you go out on visits. You wouldn't want to get that negative energy all over a patient, would you?"

"Of course not," Jim said.

He had known about Jane's Other Man from the beginning, but he hadn't known he was Sex Addict Ben. He only knew his emotional odor, which had been clinging to Jane for weeks. Jim only knew that it must be someone from the hospital, and he never tried very hard to find out anything more than that. That wasn't what he was supposed to do. He was supposed to wait for her to tell him, to trust that she would. So he pretended everything was fine.

As hard as it was, that's what he did. But he made it a little easier on himself by indulging in his own cheat. Not a sexual cheat, of course, or even an emotional one. Instead, he flirted with the idea of leaving her, and surely fantasies of abandonment were allowed while you were waiting for your wife to get brave enough to tell you she was cheating, surely he was allowed the satisfaction of punishing her, as long as he didn't hurt her. And after all, he wasn't even flirting with divorce, just with Alice.

It was a patient who had introduced them, a cranky old man on the VIP floor. That wasn't even Jim's regular beat. He was only up there for Ash Wednesday, the hospital chaplain's busiest day of the year, carrying his little pot from room to room.

"Get out!" the man yelled, when Jim strolled in to say he was the chaplain on duty, making his rounds to check on people's spirits and offer them a daub of ash. "I'm an *atheist*," the man said, hissing up the *s*, like that would scare Jim away.

"Terrific!" Jim said. "So am I."

"Really?"

"Really!" Jim said. The man, whose name was Charlie, softened his glare. He beckoned Jim to his bedside, and even let him place the ashes, once he discovered that Jim was offering circles instead of crosses. Jim's boss, a stern and remote Lutheran pastor, had finally acceded to his lobbying on behalf of all the people in the hospital who might wish to wear proof of their awareness of mortality, and a sign of their faith in *something*, but to whom crosses were anathema. So Jim went around with his little pot of ashes, in solemn joy, making crosses for the cross folk and circles for the circle folk, reminding everyone that they were going to die one day.

"Ashes to ashes," he said to Charlie, who asked for a smiley face on his bald spot instead of a circle on his forehead. "Dust to dust. From dust thou were made, to dust thou shalt return. Remember that now is all that you have, forever."

Charlie laughed. "Just this part, actually," he said, gesturing with a spotted hand at everything below his neck. "The top piece has got a lot longer."

"Excuse me?" Jim said, and Charlie explained: the application, the dewars, the glorious future.

Why the fuck would anybody do that? Jim wanted to ask, but he asked instead, "Why do *you* want to do that?" They talked for a half hour—Jim sensed a need, and he would have stayed even longer if it hadn't been the busiest day of the year, but Charlie only wanted to talk about the future, not his own ambiguous grief at the approaching end of his life. So Jim closed the visit with a prayer to the Great Spirit of Eternity, holding hands with Charlie and asking that his frozen sleep be brief, his freeze damage be minimal or nonexistent, and his life beyond life be forever flourishing.

"Amen to that shit," Charlie said, but he had tears in

his eyes. Then he asked why Jim wasn't wearing a circle or a smiley face of his own.

"Well, you don't really do it to yourself," Jim said. "But one of my colleagues will do me up later. It's like when the waiters have dinner after the restaurant closes."

"I'll do it right now," Charlie said, "if you want. I'm qualified, right? A fellow atheist?"

"Sure," Jim said. He handed over the pot and sat on the bed with his face turned up and his eyes closed.

"Ice eternal," Charlie said, making the circle in three short rough sweeps. "Life to life. Remember that you don't ever have to die."

"Except that I do!" Jim added, opening his eyes to see Charlie's wide grin. "Amen!" Jim bowed and left the room. *The patient is a citizen of Spiritual World A*, he would write in the chart (and later, in his book, as he recounted the story to no one at all, for the purpose of forgetting it utterly), meaning that he knew what he knew, spiritually, and a chaplain wouldn't do him any clinical good by sowing doubts in his mind or trying to shake up his placid unquestioning faith. *He describes himself as an atheist, but really he worships God as the Future.* Back in the pastoral care offices, Jim ran into his boss. "Jesus, Jim!" she said. "It's Ash Wednesday, not fucking Pictionary!"

"What?" he said. She raised her hand in a furious salute, one finger pointing stiffly at her forehead.

Jim went into the bathroom to see that Charlie had drawn a triangle on his head. Jim wiped it off, feeling conned. Back when he was a chaplain intern, still afraid to pray with his patients, he once bargained a sweet old lady into leading their prayer together, thinking that would allow him to avoid having to call out to anything or anybody he didn't believe in. She'd agreed, but only after he promised to repeat what she said word for word, so she tricked him into throwing himself on the mercy of Jesus, and dedicating his life to Him forever. She had grinned in just the same way that Charlie did, and Jim felt just as dirty afterward, having been sanctified to a final principle that went against everything he believed in. He wanted to go back up to Charlie's room and shout at him, to ask him if he had ever made his life mean something, if he had ever dared risk everything with another terminally human being, dared love somebody knowing in your bones that this life was all you had. But he knew that wouldn't make somebody like Charlie understand.

So I waited all day to talk to my wife, he wrote in his book. Since she was the only person—she always had been—who could really understand why his day was so upsetting. He went home early and waited for her, perusing the Polaris website so they could look at it together, covering their mouths and pointing. She texted that she would be late coming home, and as the hours passed Jim flipped back and forth between the website and the sort of tasteful porn he used sometimes to rev himself up for her, since he wanted nothing more than to erase the mark on his forehead by rubbing his face over every part of her body. *There you are, I said, when she came home,* and she smiled and said she was sorry for being late. She came over to ask what he was looking at, close enough that he could *smell* her, and then really *see* her, and understand what she had been doing. He closed his computer and said, "Nothing, really. Nothing at all."

And that's how I met Alice, he wrote. Not right away, of course. He kept on learning about Polaris, because he was still waiting to tell Jane all about it, after she told him her own news, when her fidelity finally moved her to confess her affair while confessing would still have *meant* something. The flirtation with Alice, when it started, was just something to do while Jim was waiting for Jane to come back to him. *Or else*, he wrote, *it was just a perfect complementary affair*, illusory until it wasn't, perfect because it signified a more complete withdrawal than anything she might manage. And yet, if she had only done what she had promised she would, he could have deleted his Polaris account. But instead he found her with her lover at breakfast, and two days later he went to Oviedo to sign the papers.

3

Jim stared at his neat blocky handwriting, half-expecting the words to disappear while he watched. But he never forgot what he wrote until after he closed the book, marking whatever he was working on as *finished*. He'd never flipped back the pages to see, but he expected the words were all still there, that the people and ideas they represented disappeared only from his mind, not from the page. If the words actually disappeared, then he wouldn't need to burn the book, would he?

He made another kind of note, on a single sheet of paper, adding to a list of things he wanted to ask Alice. This was a good idea in theory, but in practice it was a little more complicated, since he had no idea anymore what the questions referred to, and didn't dare look back to check. So he hadn't asked her any of the questions yet. Still, he would add this one to the list: *No. 12: Do I really have to burn the book?* Meaning, he supposed, did he really have to destroy the memories, once he had forgotten them? Maybe it was a theological distinction, to say that these people and things could be *dead to him* and yet *alive to themselves* within the pages, only waiting, like the famous cat in the box, for someone to look in before they could live and breathe again within the sacred spaces of memory. Which is perhaps something he had already considered, and what he meant when he wrote *No. 6: But what about the cat?* or possibly *No. 9: Mystic memory? Chords of memory? The whole universe as recording medium? Immortal memory? Living vs Dead = ROM vs RAM?*

"Alice!" he shouted, not closing the book yet. "Alice! Get up here!" He had discovered, in the weeks since Sondra had died, that they would tolerate all sorts of rude behavior in the house, and the only reason they hadn't brought him his meals in his room and excused him from every last social obligation before now was that he hadn't demanded it. The work was everything, Alice told him. That's what he was there for, and she was there to help in whatever way her experience and Jim's own best interest permitted her. He could have asked the house, in a much quieter voice, to pass on a message, but he preferred to shout. Shortly, she appeared at his door.

"Yes?"

"Come sit down," he said, with his finger still on the page, preparing himself to ask what he wanted to ask. He wrote it down instead, holding a finger up at her to wait. *Can't I keep this memory?* he wrote. *Since it hurts?*

"Was there something I could help you with?" Alice asked. "Would you like some tea?"

Jim stared a little longer at what he wrote, then closed the book and looked up at her. "Never mind," he said. "False alarm. Sorry."

"I am here to serve you," she said, rising and bowing.

"Wait!" he said, when she'd just passed into the hall. She came back.

"Yes?"

"I changed my mind," he said. He wanted some tea, after all.

"Good," she said. "Tea is lovely in the afternoon."

"It certainly is," he said. She left him at his desk and went to fetch it. He was crying again, but already he didn't know what for.

4

There were all of Jim's clothes to take care of. Her mother
told Jane she should just leave them as they were for a few
months. They were in their own closet, after all; she
could just shut the door. There might be the temptation,
of course, to go into the little room and cuddle with the
empty suits, to take luxuriating draughts of air flavored
with the smell of his shirts and his shoes, and this wasn't
anything to be ashamed of, her mother said. If there was
one thing that forty years of ministry had taught her
mother, it was that *no two people grieved in the same way.*
Still, she said, we all make such rooms, cabinets of the
mind into which we may retreat and imbibe like air
the memory of the beloved.

But Mr. Flanagan all but ordered Jane to empty the
closet. "Just make sure the base station is plugged in," he
said, and Wanda reminded her to make sure to write in
her journal as soon as she was done sorting the clothes.
This work was a surefire way to jack up her mental-
anguish numbers, and Flanagan said he wanted a good

run of hard data before seeking a formal injunction against Polaris. "The complaint itself will be just the prelude to a double shit-ton of supplementary material," he told her. "They'll give up before we even begin."

So Jane collected her grief button and got started one afternoon, abandoning her lunch. Her mother was cooking aggressively—mostly from scratch, but also altering the gifts of food from the hospital chaplains, sniffing and tasting other women's dishes to rehabilitate them, somehow managing to store them in the weeks after they arrived without ever again subjecting Jane to the sight of frozen meat. That day she had made a dull casserole almost delicious just by adding a little rosemary and cutting the canned tuna with fresh fish. Millicent was getting noticeably fatter, but Jane, never hungry, had lost weight, and her mother announced she would stay as long as it took to get Jane back to her usual size.

"We'll be right up to help!" her mother called out as Jane climbed the stairs, and she stared a long time at the closet door before she entered, imagining it padlocked or barred or crossed with caution tape. She held her breath as she went in, taking only a quick tasting gasp, and discovered that the little room smelled mostly of his feet, from the shoes standing in neat rows on risers along the wall. And because his feet smelled like her feet—this had not always been the case but was one of those marital convergences that she thought might have presaged their coming to look like sister and brother in old age—there was nothing nostalgic, in neither the gratifying nor the distressing sense, about the odor, and it was not something she'd be able to escape by shutting the door and running away, unless she could manage somehow to outrun her own feet.

When her mother and Millicent came up, Jane had only moved the shirts and pants and suits around from bar to bar, making hanging piles for the Salvation Army and Goodwill and the local HIV charity, trying to decide which clientele would most desire a pair of green velour tracksuits. Millicent took one from her and embraced it like a lover.

Jane sat on the floor and poked absently at Flanagan's button. Her mother kept trying to send her to bed, since she and Millicent had the project totally under control, but Jane wouldn't go. It felt more and more like being at the funeral again—watching other people bustle about on Jim's behalf while she just sat there, suspecting that none of it was any more real than a dream she kept having, in which she sat on their stoop watching a boy-size Jim licking a popsicle that was an exact replica of his head. Every night she watched him, and he watched her back with a dull, lazy look, exactly the way some wary, bored child might look at you over his ice cream. And always, eventually, he held the stick out to her, and without any hesitation at all she took a long lick up the side of the nose. It tasted like peaches.

"Look what I've found, Jane. You don't want to give *this* away." Her mother was holding a piece of heavy paper in her hands while Millicent looked over her shoulder and made a sad purr. Jane hadn't known *that* was in here. She thought Jim would have put it in the safe. "Do you remember this?" her mother asked stupidly. It was not a birth certificate or a death certificate, or even a baptismal certificate. It was more like a little crafts project, something one of the nurses had led them through after the stillbirth, the hands and feet recorded forever (or as long as paper might last) in blue-black ink.

"Oh, that . . ." Jane said, pressing her button furiously as she got up to go lie down on her bed. "You can just throw it away."

She lay facedown on the bed with her arms out beside her, utterly still except for the spasmodic clicking of her thumb, and even that died away as she remembered that Polaris had nothing to do with this particular anguish. Her mother didn't have to step out of the closet for Jane to hear her in her head: *One death recalls another, and whenever somebody dies on you, everyone you've ever lost dies again.* But it wasn't as simple as that.

5

That last almost-baby, *all* the almost-babies (not so fully formed as the last one, in his delicate and excruciating little nose and fingers and cheeks and toes, but not much less *real* for that) and also the hosts of theoretical babies, the ones they might have had or might yet have been trying for, had gathered together into a single entity, a confederated accuser who had prosecuted vigorously against the meaning of Jane's life. She and Jim had eventually, on the other side of her stupid affair, found a way to live a defense together, though Jim always had his crazy chaplain ways of thinking about it, and she had her own ways. But they hadn't had to agree on everything to make the defense work. The question now—and she started clicking vigorously again as she understood this—was how she was ever going to win this new case, when Jim, her partner, her chief counsel, her only real friend, had gone over to join the prosecution. *This has nothing to do with the baby!* she wanted to shout at her mother, who, worse than being right all the time, was always just barely wrong.

"Well, of course Jim's thinking about a baby *now*," her mother had told her, when Jane had gone up to Northampton alone to fetch the cat back, after a two-week trip to Puerto Rico to celebrate Jim getting off anticoagulants. "It's like he's finally all better. And he nearly died, didn't he? Never mind that it was nearly two years ago to you and me. To him, it was probably yesterday. A little fender bender or ten pages of Camus was always enough to make your father come at me like a *Mormon*. Just give him some time. He'll settle down. And he can't be a surgeon anymore. He's just looking for something to do with his life, isn't he?"

"But did you want one?"

"One what, dear?"

Jane rolled her eyes. "A little Mormon."

"Well, no," her mother said, looking searchingly into her tea. "Not at first. And that's all right, you know. It's just two entirely different states of existence, the before and the after of it. Neither can understand the other, but one is also not *inferior* to the other."

"I have no idea what you're saying," Jane told her. "But you know what I would never tell my child? *I didn't want to have a baby.*"

"Jane," her mother said. "You're not a teenager. If you want me to help you in your discernment, you have to let me be honest with you."

"But I don't want your help," Jane said. "I don't even

want to talk about this anymore. I just came here to get my cat!"

"Of course," her mother said. "When have you ever needed anybody's help?" She clapped her hands and called for Millicent, who did all the actual work of cat-sitting when Jane left Feathers at the house. Millicent brought the cat in, dressed up like a baby, of course, which Jane would have accused her mother of setting up somehow, if this hadn't been their first conversation about a baby, and if Millicent wasn't always dressing the animal up and e-mailing photos of Librarian Cat, Housewife Cat, or Junkie Cat. Baby Cat was just a stupid coincidence. "Oh, Millicent," Jane's mother said. "That's Jane's christening dress."

Millicent frowned and handed Jane the cat, a floppy overweight Maine coon, who lay placidly in her arms with its eyes half-closed. Jane scowled at all of them.

"She's very pretty, though," her mother said, to Millicent's quivering lip. And to Jane she said, "Doesn't it feel nice? That's all I meant, dear. You'll never really know what it means to want one, until you're actually *holding* it."

"Don't be ridiculous," she said to her mother. And she didn't throw away her birth control pills when she got home, but she did put them away someplace where they'd stay out of sight, a bathroom drawer full of old shampoo that she hadn't used in years. "Well," she said to Jim in bed that night. "Here we go, I guess."

She got pregnant right away, and lost it right away,

which she saw as a punishment for not wanting it enough, for feigning interest for Jim's sake. Soon, though, as a baby became the only thing she wanted, she grew convinced that she had in fact been feigning disinterest to herself, but this deception deserved a punishment of its own. Intellectually, that chain of reasoning was hard to sustain, but she had no trouble at all *feeling* the truth of it, through two more miscarriages and the trying and trying and trying in between.

Later she wondered if she ought to have consulted somebody before trying the first time, if she might have managed some kind of preemptive hormonal redecoration to make her body more hospitable to the little speck. She was forty-one when they started, after all. But when she asked her OB (a woman as blunt as a punch in the face) about it, she told Jane not to be stupid. "Nice try," she said, "but you can't make this your fault." How very like an OB, Jane thought, that brusque attacking kindness, catty and paranoid and defensive all at once. Jane liked it. As the losses (and the expense) mounted, people came crawling out of the woodwork, reeking of *baby*, to recommend their own doctors or fertility centers, but Jane would never have dreamed of leaving hers. Though she pretended to be comforted by Jim, her own doctor was the only person who could make her feel better about what was happening.

Of course, the doctor's awesome crankiness eventually failed her. When she gave Jane the news that the baby was dead inside her at thirty weeks, and would have to be delivered in some grotesque mockery of childbirth, it would have been so much better if she had said, *You are a useless lady, a waste of space as a body, a bad idea, even, and I hate you through and through—but none of that has anything to do with why you lost this baby.* But she was all sad sweetness during the delivery. "You're going to get through this," she kept saying confidently.

"Okay," Jane replied. "But then what?"

"Then we just do whatever comes next," Jim said. He held her hand and told her, like everybody else in that strange, subdued room, to push or not push. None of them seemed to understand that Jane might actually be giving birth to the sadness that would claim the rest of her life. *You don't even have to put me under,* she wanted to say, but just cut it out. Don't make me *participate* in this.

When the baby was out, somebody wrapped it up and put it on her chest. She wasn't entirely there for that part. One of her baby books had told her about the rush of relief and joy she would feel when the baby was born, that she should *get ready for the most indescribable feeling you will ever have.* That part held true—the terrible feeling, with the shape of elation but the substance of regret, was so hard to describe she thought it would kill her to try, so she stayed quiet and still, half out of her mind. When she awoke to the world, a nurse was there, stamping the baby's little hands and feet, performing the whole operation upon Jane's body like she was a crafts table. "What are you doing?" Jane said. "Are you booking it for a crime? Are you booking it for being dead?"

"It's just handprints and footprints," the nurse said, wincing slightly. "For the memory box."

"I said it was okay," Jim said.

"A memory box? Does it seal the memories in and keep them there forever and never let them out?"

"If you want it to," the nurse said without looking at Jane. To Jim, she said, "I've asked the chaplain to come."

"Okay," Jim said.

"Why not?" Jane asked. "Maybe he can take a picture of us with his phone."

"Jane," Jim said. "Jesus."

"Sure," she said. "He can come, too. As long as the chaplain is coming. Why is this on me? Did somebody ask me before they put it there?"

"I wanted . . ." Jim said. "I thought you would . . ."

"What am I supposed to do with it? Feed it?"

"It's a boy," he said.

"I thought we agreed we weren't going to find out about that." She turned away from him as much as she could without spilling the baby off her chest.

"Not before it was born," Jim said stupidly, but Jane only sighed.

"So what are we going to do with it?"

"I don't know," Jim said. "They'll release him to us. Or cremate him."

"Like medical waste," Jane said. "Maybe we should just put him in a coffee tin and bury it in the yard."

"Or we could have him stuffed," Jim said. "How about that? Stuffed and poseable? We could dress him up for holidays. Hell, we could put him on top of the Christmas tree!"

"Stop," she said.

"Stop what?" Jim asked. "I'm just being funny. Now we're both comedians. How's that? Maybe if we're funny enough, the baby will *laugh*."

"Now you're being cruel," she said.

"Well, you were cruel first," Jim said, and put his face in his hands. And that was how the chaplain found them. Later, Jim imagined what they must have looked like, him hiding his face, Jane turned away in bitter anger and hurt, and the purple-faced, half-swaddled baby neglected between them on her chest.

"May I come in?" the stranger asked. "I'm Dick Carver, the chaplain on call."

"All right," Jim said.

"I'm so sorry for your loss," he said to them.

"Thanks," Jane said flatly. "It's okay, though. We did some crafts."

"Oh," Dick said. "May I?" He picked up the certificate and frowned at it.

"You can have it, if you want."

"No, thank you," Dick said. "But I think I hear you. It's too much, isn't it? And not enough, at the same time." He was a little hobbit of a man, shaggy-haired and hairy-handed. Jim was sure his feet must be covered with fur.

"Sure," Jane said. When Jim took her hand she didn't pull away, but she didn't look at him, either.

"Would you like to do something else? I could do something else, if you'd like me to."

"What do you mean?" Jim asked.

"A ceremony. Something small. But sometimes it's . . ." He waved the certificate. "Often it's more than *this*. Would you like to?"

"Sure," Jim said right away. Jane rolled her eyes. "Her mother is a pastor," Jim said, as if he needed to explain why his wife wasn't being more polite. But Jane didn't take away her hand.

"My father was a pastor, too," said Dick, and then put the certificate aside and got started. Much later, he and Jim would have debates about the nature and use of pastoral authority, because Jim objected, in theory, to Dick's habit of boldly taking control of emotional horror shows in the hospital. But in practice, that early morning, it made all the difference in the world for this little man to boss them around for five minutes. He didn't take away Jim's grief, or lessen it by a single iota, but he took control of it for a few moments, which felt like enough time for Jim to get a toe back into the world.

Dick sang a psalm in Hebrew, then recited a Yeats poem about a child stolen by fairies, gently bludgeoning them with the refrain until Jane and Jim were both freely in tears. Then he asked what name they would like for the baptism.

"Baptism?" Jane said. "Like a Catholic?"

"Not into a church," Dick said. "Into your lives."

"Ralph," said Jim.

"Ralph?" Jane asked. That hadn't even been on their list of possible names.

"I don't want to use any of those names," Jim said, not saying to her (and barely saying to himself) that he wanted to save them all for the *other* babies, the ones they might still have.

Dick took a splash from a plastic water bottle and put it on the baby's tiny head. "Ralph," he said. "With water as pure as your spirit I baptize you son to your father, Jim, and son to your mother, Jane. Love created you. Love will sustain them through the loss of you. You will always be remembered." Then he asked Jim and Jane if they wanted to say something.

"Did you hear that, Ralph?" Jim sobbed. "It doesn't matter that you're dead. We love you anyway."

"Yes, it does," Jane said quietly. "Yes, it does matter. But we love you. That part's true."

Before the two of them could argue the point, Dick closed them down with another sung Hebrew prayer. He must have withdrawn sometime very soon after that, but Jim had no memory of him leaving. Jim didn't remember anything of the hour or so that followed except that when someone finally came to take the baby away, Jane held it to her chest and said, barely intelligible through her tears, "I never want to see another baby again as long as I live."

"You don't have to," Jim said. "You never do." But he of course wasn't able to protect her, in the weeks and months afterward, from the random child who pulled on her skirt in the supermarket line and said, "Hey, lady, you have pretty hair," or the trick-or-treaters who ignored his NO CANDY TONIGHT sign and rang insistently at the doorbell, or even, eventually, the sight of her patients, whose faces at least were hidden from her as they lay opened before her, half dead and half alive, on the operating table.

He couldn't even protect her from his own (deeply considered but still totally unwise) overtures toward adoption, the brochures from agencies that he left about as if by accident, or the disastrous Christmas gift of an African orphan sponsorship. He was trying so hard, and none of it helped.

"She doesn't even notice," he said eventually to Dick, after Dick had become his supervisor. Jim had enrolled in Clinical Pastoral Education courses—partly to give Jane space, partly to keep himself busy. "Or maybe she doesn't even care."

"Or maybe she doesn't understand," Dick said. "You're speaking a different language now. She's a surgeon, after all."

"So am I," Jim said.

"Not anymore," Dick said, leaning forward and staring at him in the way he had during their first week of instruction, when he said, "I am bringing all of my attention to bear on you. Your job is to be fully present for my attention." Jim laughed at him the first few times, but he found that as he learned to actually be more present, as he learned that presence was actually a skill you could practice, he found he had to cover his face with his hands after only a moment or two. It was a year before he could ever stare Dick down.

He looked away. "Now you're one of us," Dick said.

"I'm getting there, anyway," Jim said. He hadn't yet been tested in the way he knew would make him or break him. He failed the first few times, calling Dick in the middle of the night and asking him to go to the hospital in his stead, because he just wasn't ready to face those parents yet. And then, once he had gathered the courage to go into the room, he failed again, muttering uselessly at them about how they would find a way to be happy again. He cried out his tears in the hospital bathroom, so Jane wouldn't have to see them.

"But are we *parents*?" the poor father asked him, the night Jim passed the test. *I was answering for all of us*, he tried to tell Jane, who seemed too tired to listen to him, when he rushed home to let her know what had finally happened.

"Of course you are," Jim said, crying, but not out of control; overwhelmed, but not crushed, believing it for all of them in the room and for Jane, too, believing it for every stillborn parent in the world. "And now, just like for any of us who've had a child, nothing is ever going to be the same for you."

6

"That's lovely," Sondra said, leaning on one arm in her bed with one hand in her curls and one on her heart, "in a really terrible way."

"But really I had nothing to do with it," Jim said. "Everything helpful or true about the moment was in *them*. I was just the stick for the rock candy, you know?"

"I hate rock candy," Sondra said. "But I probably know what you mean. People were always telling me their troubles, in the shop. People are so stupid, most of the time." She sighed and rolled her eyes. "So all you have to do is listen to them and then when they ask you what they should do, you say, 'Don't be so *stupid*.'"

"Did you and Joe ever want to have children?" Jim asked.

"Jesus, no," she said. "Never. We thought we did, at first, but it didn't take much not getting one before we realized we were upset about not having something other people wanted *for* us. So I sat us down in the chair, so to speak, and told us to stop being so stupid."

"And Joe felt the same way?" Jim asked.

"Even more so," she said. She waved her hand. "He had this spiel about the *marriage* being a baby. About how we were lucky because everybody else was just distracted from the important thing, which was making something together that would last and last and last. What do regular babies do, anyway, but use you, and grow up, and move away, and stop calling? Then it's just the two of you again, and you've wasted all your time and love on these terrible creatures who are always going to love somebody else more than you. Ugh! He thought we were lucky because we got to skip that part."

"You *were* lucky," Jim said. "You had each other."

"Well, I could take or leave the metaphor stuff," she said. " 'Stop hurting the baby!' he said sometimes, meaning 'Don't make me want to divorce you!' Joe was the big-idea man in the business. He came up with the slogans and the business plans—I just cut the hair and recognized the bullshit. The part I liked was the idea that if we just tried hard enough, the baby would grow up one day, and unlike a horrible, selfish child, eventually the *marriage* would take care of *us*. And I suppose it did."

"But that's beautiful," Jim said.

"It did the job," she said flatly, "until now." And then they were quiet until dinner.

7

Jane edged past the lady in the aisle seat, her phone in one hand and her bag in the other, turning and half-falling into her seat by the window.

"How do you do?" the woman asked, bobbing her head and smiling. Her yellow hair sat stiffly on her head, and curled on either side of her chin into two sturdy-looking handles.

"Good," Jane said, trying to make it sound like *It's* good *to be alone on the plane* or *How* good *it is that we've decided not to talk to each other today.* Jim was the one who liked to talk to strangers. Still, she smiled at the woman, because she wasn't exactly trying to be rude. The flight attendant came over to ask if they'd like something to drink before the plane took off. Jane shook her head, but the woman ordered *du champagne.* Jane called her husband.

"You again!" he said when she answered.

"Haha," she said. "I have a couple minutes before they shut the door."

"How have you been since the last time we talked?"

"Would you stop that, please?" She had spent the whole taxi ride from Paris to the airport on the phone with him.

"Sorry," he said. "Safe flight. I love you."

"You, too," she said. "Are you at work?"

"Leaving in a minute," he said. "I'm just sitting here."

"What time will you be home?"

"Not sure. I might spend the night if it's busy."

"Oh, don't do that," she said. "Please."

"Why not?"

"Oh, Jim." The flight attendant brought Jane champagne as well, leaving it on her armrest and backing away with a smile. If she drank it, she would have to pee in an hour, defeating the purpose of dehydrating herself all day for the sake of her window seat. Her seatmate raised her own glass. "Today is the twenty-eighth, you know," Jane said.

"Is it?" he said, and then added, theatrically, "Is it?" Jane sighed. "I'm just kidding. I got us dinner reservations," he said.

"No, you didn't," she said. "You always forget this one."

"Yes, I did. And anyway, you always forget the *other* one."

"I don't *care* about the other one," she said. "You were asleep for that one. I was being crazy for that one."

"Well, I care about them both. And I did too make reservations."

"Okay," she said, deciding not to challenge him by asking where they were eating. "They're about to close the door."

"All right," he said. "I love you. Safe flight."

"I love you, too," she said.

"I'm so glad I married you. Both times."

"Me, too," she said. "I'll see you soon." She hung up and turned her phone off, then picked up her champagne glass and leaned toward the window.

"Is it your *anniversary*?" her seatmate asked breathlessly.

"Yes, it is," Jane said.

"Oh, how nice. How long?"

"Eight years," Jane said, though in fact it was eight only for the one anniversary, and nine for the other.

"Oh, what's that one? Macramé? Jute? Some kind of woven plant, I think. I can never keep track."

"Neither can my husband," Jane said.

"Mine neither," the lady said. "But he's very good with birthdays." Jane did something not totally friendly with her lips and looked away, thinking that ought to signal the end of the conversation without being rude. But the woman said, "You must love him very much."

"Sometimes," Jane said automatically, finishing her champagne in one long draw, and closing her eyes after putting the glass back on the armrest. The lady didn't ask for details, and Jane was much happier anyway continuing this conversation with herself: *Sometimes I love him so much I can hardly stand it.* Sometimes it felt like the only purpose of her life was to hurry toward him, and sometimes it felt like the only purpose of her life was to hurry away. *And isn't it like that for everyone?* she asked.

8

When Jim asked her to marry him—with a ring baked into some buttery naan at the Indian restaurant near her old Upper West Side apartment where they ate once a week during their long courtship—Jane might just have said *No* or *Not right now* or even *Can I have some time to think about this?* There were a hundred other options besides flight and silence.

She could have said *I need to be alone for a few days.* Or *I'm just going to go to the bathroom for a moment to cry.* Instead, she stared at him for a strange, timeless instant, panicked and still. Her field of vision seemed to crumble away from the periphery. Jim was making a very hopeful face—she couldn't hear anything he was saying, but the way his mouth was moving and the way his eyebrows were reaching sincerely toward the ceiling made him look like he was singing barbershop quartet at her. Then she understood that he actually *was* singing to her, and the reason that the three waiters on duty that night had clustered so close around him was that they were singing, too. She couldn't really hear the song (it was "Heart of My Heart") in the restaurant, but it would keep her up at night and become the theme song of Jim's ICU stay.

She felt *caught*, as if Jim and these three nice Indian gentlemen had opened their mouths and poured not music but accusation out upon her, casting a spotlight on her hypocrisy, her insufficient affection, her cowardice and naïveté. The music finally stopped. Everyone in the restaurant was watching, gleeful with anticipation. Without saying a word, Jane stood, carefully folded her napkin upon her seat, and left the restaurant. She walked home and got straight into the tub. She was still hiding in the lukewarm water a half hour later when Jim, after he had settled the bill and explained to all his new Indian and non-Indian friends at Indus Valley that everything was perfectly all right, was hit by a taxi turning left off Broadway onto Ninety-Ninth Street.

On the way up to the hospital she kept wondering, hysterically, if the taxi she was in was the one that had hit him, and she alternated, in her shouting at the driver, between telling him to slow down and be careful and to hurry up. She rushed up there only to find she couldn't even see him—the trauma surgeon threw her out of the OR. She had to stay in the waiting room, like a civilian. "But they have to let me help fix him," she said calmly to the scrub nurse who hustled her out and stayed with her all during the first surgery, who didn't leave her side until Jim was recovering in the surgical ICU. She sat Jane down in a chair by Jim's bed, and that's where Jane stayed.

That's where her mother and Millicent found her when they arrived. Jane held Jim's hand and glared at the monitors for week after week, he never emerging from his coma, she never emerging from her quiet hysteria, until she finally understood what she had to do.

"I want us to get married," Jane said at last, when Jim had been in the ICU for three weeks.

"That's wonderful," said Millicent. "Do you hear that, buddy?" she said to Jim, leaning down to shout in his ear. "I told you she'd come around."

"Good, dear," said her mother, giving Jane a hug. "That's *very good.*"

"Right now," Jane said, not hugging her back. Her mother stiffened. Millicent frowned.

"But Jim's not awake yet," her mother said.

"And he won't be," Jane said. "Not until we're married."

"Darling," her mother said. "That's just trauma and superstition talking." She held Jane at arm's length.

"It's not superstition," Jane said. "It's what I *feel.*"

"Exactly," her mother said. "And even if we could find someone to do the ceremony, how could Jim say yes?"

"He already did," Jane said. "Do you think I don't know what he said? And you can do the ceremony."

"Jane," her mother said. "You're not being rational about this."

"You are going to do this for me!" Jane shouted, clutching at her mother's shoulders and squeezing them until she could feel her bones.

"Let's just have a confab," Millicent said gently, untangling the two of them and taking Jane's mother outside. They came back pretty shortly. "First things first," Millicent said. "We need to see about a dress for you."

It was easy enough to arrange. Jim wasn't brain-dead, but nobody on the ICU team thought he was ever going to wake up. His poor brain had completed its heaving sigh, swelling up and then down, and now he was just lying there. Collegiality made Jane's fellow physicians a little brutal with her (*I'm going to tell it like it is, Jane*, they'd say, *because I know you can take it*), but it also afforded her some autonomy.

They did it as soon as Jane could change her clothes— Millicent found her a white tracksuit in the gift shop. Jim's nurse was Jane's witness, Millicent was Jim's. Not that they needed witnesses. It didn't have to be official in that way. The room was already full of flowers, but the only music they could get was a music thanatologist who had just finished harping somebody into the next life in the palliative care suite down the hall, but she could play "Heart of My Heart" after Jane hummed a few bars.

"Dear friends," her mother began, and then launched into an extemporaneous sermon about the nature of *divine surprise*. Jane wasn't listening. She had too much to say to Jim, and she knew that time was running out. *I'm so sorry*, she told him. *I didn't know what I felt, but now I know what I feel.* "Do you, Jane Julia Cotton," her mother was asking her, "take this man to be your wedded husband, to have and to hold from this day forward, for better for worse, for richer for poorer, in sickness and health, to love, cherish, and worship, until death do you part, according to God's holy ordinance?"

"Yes," Jane said. "Hurry up!"

Her mother asked the corresponding question of Jim, and Millicent leaned down next to him as if to listen for his whispered reply. "He does," she said. Jane's mother told her she could kiss the groom, so she bent down to do it. "Careful!" the nurse whispered, anxious for his ventilator tube, but Jane was exquisitely gentle. With the tube in the way she couldn't press both her lips to his, but she caught his lower lip in a sort of dry hug with her mouth. She thought it would be enough.

Then everybody but the bride and groom wept gently, and the music thanatologist played the wedding march, as if Jane was going to pull up the cuffs of her sweatpants and rush in merry ecstasy out of the ICU and the hospital. "Now wake up," she said to him in tears, "so I can tell you how happy I am," but really she was afraid he might just roll over and die.

He didn't die, but he didn't wake up, either. He just lay there, same as ever, for another two months, at which point he opened one eye and peered around the room, then closed it again. He did that for a couple of weeks, that single open eye like the periscope of his consciousness taking the lay of the world above to decide if it was safe to come up yet.

The first thing he noticed, when he woke up fully, was how weak he was. He could barely lift his hands to look at them, and he noticed how much heavier the left was than the right before he saw his wedding ring. "Look at that," he croaked, and Jane turned around from where she was digging through a bag. Then, in an instant, he knew he was in the ICU, and could guess that he had had an accident. For some reason he thought it would be funny to play a joke on Jane, so he said, "Who are you?"

That was a terrible idea. He'd never seen her cry so hard, or so despondently. *Thirty seconds into my second chance, and I'm already fucking up!* he thought, and then he was asleep again, exhausted by the effort of raising his hands to embrace his wife, which was what Jane kept calling herself.

"But we'll get married again," she said, "so it's real."

"Sure," he said. "We'll get married every day."

"Well," she said. "It was pretty emotional. I don't think I can handle it more than once a week."

"That'll do," Jim said. He pulled so weakly at her, he didn't even know if she would feel it, but she came closer. "This is going to be totally awesome," he said.

"Yes," she said. "I know."

But Jim still had months of rehab to get through, and it would be just over a year before they finally got married again. "We've become citizens of the ICU," he said to Jane over and over in the last week of his stay in the hospital.

"You're not in the ICU anymore."

"You never really leave a place like that," Jim said, sniffing his arm. "I'm going to smell like a hospital forever. I never smelled like a hospital when I just worked here. I've become one of those sad stories."

"No, you're not," Jane said.

"Yes, I am," Jim said. "I'm a sad *story*, but not a sad person. I'm a very happy *person*. Do you know what I mean?"

"I do," Jane said, leaning down to kiss him. "I'm happy, too." There was a knock on the door, and a man came in smiling.

"Good morning," he said. "I'm one of the chaplains. Would you like to chat?"

"Go fuck yourself," said Jim, with a little salute.

The chaplain bowed and returned the salute, then withdrew from the room. Jane watched him go, eyes wide.

"Don't worry," Jim said. "He told me I could say that. He comes by every day, and I tell him to fuck off. We have an understanding." Which was true. Jim had told the man he could come see him every day, and in return the man had told Jim he could dismiss him any way he liked. "You can't really tell the doctor or the nurse to fuck off," he had said, laying a warm palm on Jim's arm. "But you can tell me to fuck off anytime you like."

9

Jim couldn't remember the chaplain's name, but he liked to think it had been Dick, way back in his intern years. Dick said it couldn't have been him, because it was never his style to let someone tell him to fuck off every day. "You don't understand," Jim said. "We had an understanding!" And he imagined sometimes, a little wistfully, the conversation he and Dick might have had during those weeks in rehab when Jim was getting ready for his wedding—though it would be another whole year before it was all arranged—learning to walk down the aisle, and button a tuxedo shirt, and speak his vows in a clear, strong voice. "Maybe I wouldn't have had to wait five years to figure out I wanted to be a chaplain. And I think if I had been a chaplain sooner it would have made me a better husband."

"You always get everything backwards," said Dick. "It's being a better husband that makes you a better chaplain." They were in one of the pastoral care offices, alone since it was a Saturday afternoon and they were the only two chaplains on duty. Jim was looking for a car service to go fetch Jane from the airport that night and bring her to the restaurant.

Jim was about to argue with Dick some more, but then his pager went off. Dick held out his hand. "I'll take that. Go get your wife some flowers. And not from the gift shop, either." They left the office together, then split off, Dick heading left toward the main hospital and the ICUs, and Jim walking down the long hall toward the Broadway exit. He thought he should go home, since he suddenly felt too full of his own story, too eager to tell some stranger about his fragile and unbreakable marriage, to minister properly to anybody. He called Jane just to leave a message: *I can't wait to see you tonight.*

By the time he reached the end of the hall, he had regained some of his confidence. He said to himself, *I am going to bring my love for my wife into every room I visit today.* He waved to the guard at the door and passed through, into the foyer. He stopped at the second set of double doors, almost into the afternoon sunshine. A lady was walking through the doors in the opposite direction, but she paused when she saw his face.

"Whoa," Jim said, putting a hand to his chest, feeling a strange poke at the heart. "What's *that?*"

CYCLE THREE

"Come here much?" Jim whispered to Millicent, while they were waiting at the altar for Jane and her mother. He was trying not to look at all the people in the church. He couldn't tell his side from Jane's side all of a sudden, or remember if they had decided to segregate the guests like that.

"Stop talking," Millicent said through her smile. "People will think you're having second thoughts." When he had asked Jane's mother a week before if it might not be bad luck to have a second wedding, she had replied that it was *perfectly normal* to want to cancel the wedding. It was *perfectly normal* to want to run away. Ponderously, she gave him permission to have those feelings, and after that Millicent started telling him, whenever she could lean in discreetly at his ear, how all sorts of things were *perfectly normal* to feel in the run-up to the ceremony. It was *perfectly normal*, she said, to want to make a murder plan for each guest, or to wish the cake could be full of beetles, and it was *perfectly normal* to wish you could be married by a big red dildo instead of a priest.

He started to giggle as they waited, and Millicent pinched him. "Nobody's even looking at us," he whispered, which was true. Everyone had turned to watch the bride coming down the aisle. Jane looked very tall next to her mother. A trick of the light made the veil opaque, and for a moment it looked to Jim like Jane had a fancy silk bag over her head, or like someone had wrapped up her face for the morgue.

Millicent pinched him again, much more gently. She was the only person in the church looking at him instead of at Jane, but already the heads were swiveling around toward him. "Everything will be fine as soon as you see her face," Millicent said, and kissed Jim's cheek. Then she took a step back with her sister and stood behind him. He and Jane couldn't decide who to ask to be in the bridal party—they were both only children and had no close friends but each other—so they didn't ask anyone. Millicent and Marilynne were their best people.

He hadn't been anxious at all about the wedding— they were already married, so wasn't this one just for show? But now he was terrified. All of a sudden he wanted a little more time, just enough for somebody—Jane, if she could make herself available right now, or Millicent, or even a random stranger—to tell him a few dozen times that everything was going to be okay.

We are already married, Jim kept telling himself, and then, *It's perfectly normal for the groom to shit himself.* But after he raised the veil and saw Jane's apprehensive and exultant face, and as the priest went through the first part of the ceremony, he came to know, without having to hear it from anyone, that there was absolutely nothing to worry about. He didn't say to Jane, *Oh, that's right—I love you*, though that seemed, in the moment, like it would be better to say that than the vows they'd written together. Certainly it would have been *easier* to say. He didn't forget the vows—they'd decided it would be classier to memorize them—but he was so nervous he could barely pay attention to what he was saying. He and Jane spoke simultaneously, looking each other right in the face, and the looking turned out to be very hard. It felt like the first time in his life he'd ever looked somebody in the eye and said something that he meant. He'd been given so many wedding warnings and so much wedding advice, and yet no one had warned him about this. He felt like he should be very quiet when he spoke, and like he should shout, and like he should put a hand to Jane's cheek, and like he should choke her throat for passion. All these promises they were speaking had sounded sweet and prudent when they hashed them out at the dinner table, but now they were ambitious, exalted, and *scary*. The priest gave them permission to kiss each other.

"I love you," Jim said, in a daze. He was worried that he had somehow neglected to mention that in the vows. "I love you," she replied, because she was masterful like that—omitting the "too," declaring by the omission that nobody ever really went first in love, the "too" was only an accident of time, not a cause and an effect, not two causes in search of an effect. It was a causeless effect.

They had agreed not to use any tongue for the kiss, settling on something passionate and chaste, a *Gone with the Wind* sort of kiss, mouths open as if they might start trading breath, held for five seconds, which they both agreed was long enough to give people a little thrill. When they had stopped to consider it, they had both liked the idea of making the people watching them a little horny. But Jim hadn't considered they might do that to themselves. And of course it was normal, opening an interior eye during the kiss, to see a future together, to measure the time in apartments or houses or cats or even children. Jim's daze was lifting, the vows were coming back to him. That's what the kiss is for, he told himself. To have a little time to think together about all those marvelous and terrifying things you just said. They had sworn to remain *always together* and *never apart*. Not in any way that matters. *Occasionally straying, maybe*, Jim said to himself now, *but always returning, until we die.* He saw that, too: advanced old age spent hand in hand on a sun-dappled park bench and then mindless decay into matched graves.

As they kissed, Jane saw the past, the little accidents of fate (parallel schedules in medical school, coincidentally matching to the same hospital for residency) and the big accident of cheated fate that had brought them here, standing too long in their marriage kiss and using too much tongue in front of a hundred strangers and her mother and Millicent. None of them ought to see this. Not even Millicent, who had taught Jane to kiss, inspecting the motions of Jane's tongue as she made out with a clear plastic bag and composing mnemonics by which Jane might remember how to be a thoughtful and surprising lover of a boy's mouth. *Maybe we are holding this kiss too long?* Jane said to herself, exulting at the same time, in a hope like knowledge, that the kiss was never going to end.

"We kissed too long, didn't we?" Jane asked Jim in the limousine on the way to the reception, which they held at an arts club not very far from where Jim had been run over by the taxi. Jane's mother had instructed the limo driver to take the long way there, and avoid passing that particular corner.

"We sure did," he said. "Let's do it again right now."

"Not just yet," she said. At the reception she polled the few people she thought would be honest with her. "Just a little," her new friend Maureen said. "It was a *little* vulgar, sure. But it made me jealous, you know. I wish somebody had kissed me like that at my wedding. Anybody at all. Even the priest!" "Don't be stupid," said Millicent. "If you start regretting sexy kisses, then I don't even want to talk to you anymore." And Jane's mother said, "Of course it was." They were dancing together— her mother was being her father and Millicent was being her mother with Jim, a few feet away. "And of course I blushed for you. And if I had been the officiant I would have given a prearranged signal to let you know. Because it's hard to remember when to stop. But do you know what I tell newlyweds when they ask me that question?"

"That they fucked up? That they have to do it all over again? That they're not actually married?"

"That it's good luck," her mother said, kissing her cheek and passing her off to Jim. Jane could tell he was getting worn out already by the way he hung on her shoulders. He was still easy to tire, and when he drank his coordination started to slip.

"We fucked up with that kiss," Jane said. "My mother said we have to do it over again."

"Hooray," he said, and kissed her. But she drew back, saying she couldn't dance and kiss at the same time. She said that again, a few minutes later at the end of the dance, and again when they sat down, and again around the cake-cutting. "Come on," Jim said, pretty drunk by now. "Let's make out a little. We can slide under the table, if you're worried about people watching us."

"You're too tired," she said. "But it's too bad I don't still have my veil." It really would have been nice to put it down again. They ought to let you do that at your wedding, just pull down the shade for a few moments of privacy and contemplation, since she was barely getting to pay proper attention to her own wedding. The strangers— why had she invited all these strangers?—kept coming up to talk at her, so she'd had no time to decide if the salmon was too wet or too dry, or whether the wine was any good, or if she liked the signature wedding cocktail they'd paid five hundred dollars for somebody to think up and then write down on a little card to go into the favor bags. "Are you having a good time?" Jim kept asking her, and she kept saying, "I think so!" or "Probably!"

or "I'll tell you in an hour when I catch up to myself!" *At least I paid attention to the kiss*, she told herself.

But when they were finally alone again, standing in their stained and rumpled finery at the apartment door, she found herself unready. "Maybe we should go to a hotel, after all," she said. "Maureen was right. We shouldn't come home again until after the honeymoon."

"Too late," Jim said, his hand already on the door-knob. "What's wrong?"

She knew it was silly to avoid making out with your newly recertified husband just because you were afraid it wasn't going to be as good as the wedding make-out. *It's perfectly all right if it's all downhill from here*, she said to herself, and started kissing him while he was still fiddling drunkenly with the lock.

Don't compare! she told herself. She kissed him thoughtfully, tentatively, and found it to be exactly the same. It brought her right back to the wedding kiss, and once she was there, she realized that it was the *audience*, not she or Jim, that was at risk of humiliation, that she and Jim might be making their guests feel bad about their own inaugural kisses, their own relationships. Happiness in love, she thought, like obscene wealth or an ostomy bag, ought to be tastefully concealed. She and Jim ought to be up there in smartly tailored but very plain love, love that had a pool but no poolhouse, no-logo love. Anything else had to be bad luck. Anything else, the universe would punish one day. She knew all these things, but she didn't stop.

And just like Jim, as they wedding-kissed, she took

the time to consider what they had just said to each other, since she'd also been too anxious to really pay attention, a few minutes before, when she was actually speaking the vows. *Always together*, she had sworn with him, *never apart*. Maureen had said they ought to surprise each other with their vows, but Jane knew that was a terrible idea. She hated surprises. Every surprise of her life so far had been a bad one. And Jim's vows weren't just gifts, after all. Neither were Jane's own. They were a contract. They were a promise not to fuck things up, which could mean something only if the two of them explicitly acknowledged, in the vows themselves, the ways in which they had already fucked up.

Or at least the way that she had fucked up. *Always together, never apart*. But what that meant for her was: *I won't run away again. Whatever happens, no matter how scared I am, I'll wait it out with you.* She had time, as the wedding kiss went on and on, to look squarely at their last Indian dinner, at her own behavior. When they sat down, she was already afraid, though not because she was expecting Jim to propose to her. She would have behaved better if she'd been expecting it.

But all she had was a feeling that something terrible was going to happen. Jim had been making her uneasy all day long, encroaching aggressively on her bed space in the morning even though they'd already resigned themselves to the fact that she was a nighttime cuddler and he a morning one, then paging her all day long just to ask her dreamily what she was doing now, and finally wanting to hold her hand on the sidewalk even when they were walking against the stream of commuters going up Broadway. She had walked ahead of him, still holding his hand, so it must have looked for all the world that she was leading him like a child.

"Don't you like your tikka?" he asked.

"It's lovely," she said. "I don't know what's wrong with me today. Sorry if I'm being horrible."

"You're not being horrible. Have some naan. It's right out of the oven. Take some."

"But I don't think I'm even hungry," she said, shrinking away when he thrust it at her. When he didn't take it back, she tore off a piece and put it in her mouth. Now all the waiters were looking at them, and some were walking to the table. "Oh," she said when she bit the ring, "there's a rock in the bread." The staff rushed in—to help her, she thought, but they gathered around Jim as he lurched to one knee and then they all began to sing.

> *Heart of my heart, I love you*
> *Life would be naught without you*

Jim had taken her hand. She held on to his as long as she could, perfectly in control of her clutching fingers even if it felt like the rest of her body, which was already straining to run away, belonged to someone else. She was full of questions for Jim—*Why do I feel accused by this proposal? Where do their thick Indian accents go when these gentlemen sing?*—but he was too busy, too caught up with his own question, for her to ask him any of her own.

Light of my life, my darling
I love you, I love you

If she had stayed at the table, those lyrics might have become Jim's vows, since, sentimental as the words were, they said just what he felt. These waiters might have been his groomsmen in their matching black suits. Even now, their accompaniment was the only thing that kept Jim singing instead of lapsing into barking sobs.

I can forget you never
From you I ne'er can sever
Oh, say you'll be mine forever

It was plain, after she had gone, that she had not disappeared in a fit of unbearable happiness. "Everything will be very good still," the hostess kept telling Jim, though his barbershop companions all looked like they'd just seen a murder, and the other patrons had already turned away to try to look like they weren't talking about him. Without him asking, the staff packed up their dinner to go, adding gifts of food, enough for a feast. He had ten pounds on each arm when he walked out. They'd even wrapped up the mukhwas he'd asked that he and his fiancée be showered with, like wedding rice, as they left. The boys had been supposed to sing them out.

Everything is going to be fine, he kept telling himself as he trudged along to Jane's apartment. "Everything is going to be very good still." He said it in the Indian hostess's voice because he was afraid he'd be a fool to say it in his own, but after only a few repetitions he started to almost believe it. There was a version of this story, he knew, where he ran now, too, and before they could marry, they divorced over his hurt feelings. And there was another version in which Jane simply never calmed down, in which she kept asking for one more week alone until it was twenty years later and they were both married to other people. But he knew that they wouldn't choose either of those versions. Jane had only given them something to try hard at, a place to practice at the extraordinary work of being together. Running away wasn't a *no*. It was just as close to *yes* as she could get right now. Jim was smiling, shocked and pleased at what he had just made himself understand, when the cab ran him over.

Much later, he liked to tell himself he got a look at their future during the accident, that the absolute certainty of *that cab is going to hit me* became, while he was up in the air, surrounded by levitating pools of curry and dal, *Wow, you can see everything from up here!* and then a glimpse of something else. Of course, the accident had wiped out anything he might have been actually thinking or knowing or seeing right then, but real or not real, that floating moment stayed with him for the rest of his life, a nostalgic presentiment. So later, at their second wedding, the one he was awake for, in the great actual *now* of the kiss Jim thought he could see his own dumb face, heartbroken and hopeful and amazed, staring slack-jawed at them from the past.

Hang in there, he told his gaping, tumbling face.

Everything will be different, but nothing will change. That's the part that you already have, get it? The thing that doesn't change. He could feel the nonimaginary people watching as well. He felt their jealous disdain as his own good fortune. He didn't mind it at all, or care that he and Jane might be holding the kiss too long. *All together now, boys!* he called out, and they replied in a chorus, every Jim he'd been and every Jim he'd ever be, *Always together, never apart. Everything will be different, but nothing will change.*

He knew it wouldn't end, this affirming and reaffirming. Twice every year he'd do it, at the anniversary of each of his weddings, staring into a mirror and asking the nearest Jim to pass it back. *Tell them all not to worry. Everything is indeed different, but indeed nothing has changed.* Then some years he forgot. And some years he wasn't even sure if it was true anymore, so those sad hopeful fuckers in the mirror got long speeches, accusations and rebuttals instead of recited vows. And then, eventually, at last, he would say: *All's well, more or less. I love her. I don't still love her. I just love her. Same as always, my dudes.*

"What are you doing in there?" Jane called out.

"Nothing!" he said. "Brushing my teeth!"

"Are you coming to bed?"

"Right now!" He gave his teeth a few swipes, and rinsed his mouth. He fixed his hair and smoothed his mustache. Peering closer at his face, he noticed how unevenly the hairs fell across his lip, so he clipped them with scissors. All this, though she had already made it dark in the bedroom.

"Are you all right?" she asked.

"Yes, coming!" But he did a few quick, quiet push-ups, to plump up his biceps, because she always noticed, even in the dark, when they were a little bigger than usual.

"There you are," she said, when he came to bed. "I'm so sleepy."

"What time is your flight?"

"Evening," she said. "But I'm taking an afternoon case for Maureen, so I'll have to leave right from the hospital. Are you working?"

"No," he said. "But I'll come up and say goodbye."

"Oh, don't," she said. "Let's do it now. Bye bye!" She kissed him and laid her head on his chest. He could hear her softly spitting out mustache fragments. He ought to have washed his face after trimming.

"Happy almost-anniversary," he said.

"Oh, tomorrow is the eighteenth," she said. "But that one doesn't count. I was crazy. You were asleep."

"Of course it counts," he said. "What did you think I would have said, if I was awake?"

"You could have said anything."

"Maybe I wouldn't have woken up at all, if you hadn't done it."

"Let's not even talk about that. Let's talk about the other wedding." Jane ran the numbers in her head, afraid suddenly that she'd still be in Paris on the anniversary of the church service, which had followed that of the ICU service by ten days and a year.

"Sure."

"What should we do? Do you want me to make a dinner reservation?"

"I'll do it," he said.

"You'll forget. You always do."

"I don't know what you're talking about. I never forget."

She put her head back on his chest. "I'm sorry I married you while you were sleeping," she said.

"I'm so glad you did."

"Me, too," she said.

"Glad and sorry?" he said.

"Yes," she said, meaning that it was a nice, durable sort of glad, but she didn't have to explain that to him. She kissed him again. "Should we?" She shouldn't even have asked, she knew. She ought to have just taken off her nightshirt, as if it were making her uncomfortable all of a sudden, and then snuggled back up to him.

"Do you want to?"

"Yes," she said. "But I'm so tired. What if we make out a little?"

"Instead?"

"No. Maybe. Let's see what happens."

"If you fall asleep while I'm kissing you, it will hurt my feelings."

"Well, I won't do *that*."

"All right, then."

"All right."

"I love you."

"I love you."

Good night! Jane kept thinking as they kissed in the

dark, and, when it seemed certain that they had kissed their way past midnight, *Happy anniversary!* And though she didn't fall asleep, her mind wandered in that way it had when she was really exhausted, and a few times she felt like she was falling and startled against him, but she was always careful to shudder, in real pleasure, right away, so Jim wouldn't know she was wandering the twilight borderland of dreamtime, tethered by his tongue to the waking world. In just another moment she'd either be fast asleep or straddling him.

Everything will be different, she heard. *And nothing will change. How nice that we can still do this.* She meant the slow drag of tongue over tongue. Neither of them had developed mouth cancer. Or lost their teeth. Neither of them really tasted any different than they ever did before. And, not to compare, but she compared. *Don't look back,* she told herself, *just be here right now.* But she looked back, and she knew that, with no effort at all, she could slip into a dream of their marriage, a kiss without end, all their kisses in one. Hadn't there been that commercial, once upon a time, in which a bride and groom kissed so long the guests all wandered off and the janitor had to clean around them when he closed up the church? Surely, she had always thought, they would have proceeded to fucking by then. She thought the commercial was for gum. Though maybe it was for a watch.

Who are all you people, anyway? she wanted to ask the crowd, but it would have meant stopping the kiss. What did they come to see? Were they still looking? Were some of them reading the program? *Always together, never apart. I won't ever run away.* Maureen had tried to talk Jane into giving the wedding a title like *Eternity* or *Quintessence*, but Jane thought that was ridiculous, and Millicent, when she heard about that, said they should call it *The Mill on the Floss* or *Behind the Green Door*. But Jane had allowed Maureen to print up the vows, within a filigreed border, on the program, which listed the hymns and poems they'd all spent the last hour singing and speaking together.

How many vows did they need, to make this work? As many as it took to bind posterity to their love as they felt it right now. "Jesus," Jim said. "It's like trying to write a constitution." Eighteen was ridiculous, but that was just brainstorming. Nine was still too many—they had to put some faith in the future. Could three be enough? "Probably," said Jane. "But let's not count them." Because it was really just one thing they were promising, which was to stay, stay, stay. "I want to be together with you always, so I'll never stay apart from you for long. Though everything will be different, I promise you nothing will change." Every moment of this life, I'll love you. Even beyond death, I'll love you.

"So very nice," said Maureen, of the whole set of promises, once they were printed up and ready for Jim and Jane to share with a world of strangers, with a church full of people who didn't matter. "So difficult," said her mother, shaking her head, but admiringly, Jane thought. "Big promises," said Millicent. "Did we get it right?" asked Jim, and then he said, "I think we got it right." They kissed and they kissed and they kissed. "What time is it?" Jane asked. "Am I awake? Are the people still watching?" Somebody was chanting, after all, not very distinctly, but she understood the words: *Always together, never apart. I'll never stay apart from this moment for long. I promise you everything, but everything will change. I'll love you every moment of this life, but everything will change, even beyond death, and nothing will be different, never apart, and everything will change, every moment of this life, and nothing will change, even beyond death, and everything will be different, always together, and nothing will be different, even beyond death, and everything will change, every moment of this life, and nothing will change, never apart, and everything will be different, always together, and nothing will be different, even beyond death, and everything will change, every moment of this life, and nothing, absolutely nothing, will ever change.*

Also by Chris Adrian and available from Granta Books
www.grantabooks.com

THE GREAT NIGHT

'Bewitching . . . This magical and fearless work is a near-blueprint of what a novel ought to be' *Observer*

It is Midsummer's Eve and three heartbroken lovers are trapped in San Francisco's Buena Vista Park: the verdant home of Titania and Oberon's embattled court, the stage-set of a homeless theatre troupe and the lair of the malevolent, vengeful Puck. When Titania, collapsing under the weight of her own recent grief, sets Puck free, all hell – quite literally – breaks loose, and the three ill-fated mortals must survive a night of strange and monstrous wonders.

Chris Adrian has created a singularly playful, moving and humorous novel – a story that effortlessly crosses the borders between reality and dreams, suffering and magic, and mortality and immortality.

'A fabulous, crazy, imaginative journey' *Daily Telegraph*

'Beguiling, troubling and undeniably potent . . . His writing is evocative and unsettling in equal measure . . . Adrian gets under your skin and stays there' *Independent on Sunday*

Also by Chris Adrian and available from Granta Books
www.grantabooks.com

GOB'S GRIEF

'Splendid, ambitious and heartbreaking' *The Times*

When Gob's twin brother Tomo is killed in battle during the American Civil War, young Gob devotes himself to building a vast machine that will bring Tomo – indeed, all the Civil War dead – back to life. As his obsession deepens he attracts a host of drifters; a brilliant surgeon, a suffragette, and the forlorn poet Walt Whitman, all of whom have lost someone they love. But the abolition of death and the success of the machine may come at a price more hideous and awful than any of them can know.

'Remarkable . . . utterly different. A work unlike any that has come before it' *Economist*

'A rich concoction of genres and parts, a profound, life-giving elixir, the very stuff of the imagination itself . . . [it is] not so much a novel as a sheer outpouring of writing, an overflow of history, fantasy and fiction' *Guardian*

'Impressive, beautifully written . . . So much more ambitious and profound than most contemporary American fiction' *Washington Post*

'The magic and machinery in *Gob's Grief*, its overlapping story lines and its parade of colourful characters are all unforgettable, but they'd be mere smoke and mirrors without Adrian's haunting prose and his piercing understanding of love and sacrifice' *Salon*

Also by Chris Adrian and available from Granta Books
www.grantabooks.com

THE CHILDREN'S HOSPITAL

'Playful, very funny, moving, and quite unlike anything
I've read so far this century' *Guardian*

A hospital is preserved, afloat, after the Earth is flooded
beneath seven miles of water. Assailed by mysterious
forces, doctors and patients are left to remember the world
they've lost and to imagine one to come, while in their
midst a young medical student finds herself gifted with
strange powers and a frightening destiny.

'[Adrian] is an eloquent anatomist of loss . . . the genius of
his writing lies in its compassion, its ability to make what
is broken whole again. To read him is to be understood'
Julie Orringer

'Remarkable . . . In what may be a terminally sick world,
it's good to have a doctor in the house' *Washington Post*

'A work of ambition, imagination and strange beauty'
Financial Times

'Quirky, flippant and clever' *Sunday Herald*

Also by Chris Adrian and available from Granta Books
www.grantabooks.com

A BETTER ANGEL

'A gifted, courageous writer, with this collection Chris
Adrian continued to take far-reaching risks'
New York Times

Loss, whether from grief or love, regret or mourning,
weaves its way through *A Better Angel*, threading together
an intricate pattern of what we mean by that mysterious
word, mortal. Dazzling and inventive, these bold short
stories showcase Chris Adrian's endless inventiveness and
wit, and confirm his growing reputation as one of our
most exciting and unusual literary voices; a master of
heartbreaking, magical and darkly comic tales.

'Strange, beautiful, and unforgettable. Like Kafka, Poe,
and Salman Rushdie, Adrian knows the best way to
bring the miraculous to life is to write it realistically'
Boston Globe

'Astonishing' *San Francisco Chronicle*

'A lovely, potent new story collection . . . through wit
and furious inventiveness [these stories] earn our trust
and achieve a hypnotic grace' *Elle*